THE DOGS
OF ELLON

A Novel

By

Peter Lavery

For all dogs, everywhere...

Prologue

A baby boy in a tiny garden pulled at a tablecloth. It was an action that would change the sleepy town of Ellon forever.

Sander and Brithe had brought the boy into the world eleven months previous. He was starting to crawl and explore. He was an adventurous little boy.

On that day, Brithe had watched it happen like it was through a glass screen.

Completely unaware of the chain reactions that were to follow. Unknowingly, that baby's pudgy hand declared war.

The plate of food fell, crashing loudly as it hit the grass.

Sander had just returned home from his workshop. He had the toughest, grittiest hands a man could have. The wood he chiselled into tables, chairs and beds gave him the worst of splinters. On that fateful day, he had been sat on the decking, bathing his hands in a bowl of warm, salty water. A bottle of cold ale sweated next to him.

Brithe ran out onto the grass to scold the boy, who sat crying at the sudden bang of the plate on the floor.

It had been one of the warmer days of spring. That's the only reason Brithe had eaten her supper outside.

It wasn't usual for her to have the wooden fold-away table sitting in the middle of the garden like an invitation to the wild.

There had only been scraps left, but enough to catch the attention of what lay in the bushes.

Its dark eyes watched Brithe clear away the mess.

Its teeth, like mini white knives, ready for an attack.

Brithe never spoke of what happened next.

Sander, however, after too many ales, would often recount the story to anyone that would give him an ear.

The mutt came out of the darkness like a vile beast, and before we could do anything, it had its dagger teeth in him.

The baby probably died instantly.

At least, the townspeople of Ellon wished he had.

The king had written to Sander and Brithe and hoped for just that too. He didn't write it so directly.

May God have given him a swift, painless end, he said delicately in the letter. A soft way to say that he hoped the little boy didn't feel the sharp teeth for long.

Neither Brithe nor Sander could do anything to save their son. The dog had slunk from the shadows, following the smell of the fallen food, grabbed at the scraps and, in one quick motion, sunk its teeth into the baby.

By the time Sander had managed to run from the decking out to the grass, the dog had pulled the boy into the bushes and onto another life.

'Why did you not grab him?' Sander spat. Brithe, sat numbly on the grass, in a daze.

'Are you deaf?!' Sander screamed, running towards the bushes. Hoping the baby lay injured behind the foliage. But there was no baby. A tiny piece of fabric about the size of a penny was snagged on the dark green bush.

The last that remained of their son.

That day was a cruel turning point in Ellon and the surrounding towns. For too long, they had cursed the wild dogs. They were beasts. They ate raw meat, they savaged wildlife. And now. They'd eaten a baby.

The king declared a pardon for anyone who killed a dog. It was no longer against the law to find them and slaughter them. The people of Ellon had waited long enough for this. They were hungry for blood.

Someone needed to be blamed.

'If they kill us, why can't we kill them?' the town's mob had cried.

The King realised that if he himself were to avoid lynching, he'd have to allow the killings.

A once quiet town by the sea became a war zone.

Humans against dogs.

Man's worst enemy.

Sander and Brithe left their house with the big garden and reclused to an apartment just off of the main street in Ellon.

A place on a cobbled street without a garden.

An apartment above a shop. Off ground level.

Years later, they had another little boy and kept him inside. Far away from the dogs.

1.

Kace had few friends. Home-schooling did that to a boy. Wyeth, the baker's son, was his closest friend. The only trip he was allowed to make on his own was down the wooden steps, out onto the cobbled street and across the road to the bakery.

'Would you care to try our fruit loaf?' Wyeth asked Kace, as he ran his finger along the wicker baskets filled with loaves of crusty bread. 'It's fresh today,' he added.

Kace nodded and took a bite of the thick-sliced fruit loaf. The outside was hard but with a soft crunch, and the inside was as fluffy as Kace imagined a cloud to be. The odd pop of a raisin or a cranberry exploded in his mouth. This was the most exciting part of his week.

'It's nice,' Kace said, savouring every sensation.

Crunch, fluff, pop.

And he went again.

Crunch, fluff, pop, pop.

There were two raisins that time.

'My Da says it's the best fruit loaf on this side of the Royal River,' the baker's son declared proudly. 'Although he did make it, so he might be tooting his own trumpet a bit.'

Kace handed over the coins his mother had given him and took a fresh loaf from the wicker basket nearest to the stove. This was where the freshest bread was, the baker's son had once told him. And his mother deserved only the freshest loaf of bread. She was very sick, after all. If Kace could at least do this for her, maybe she'd feel so strong that her body would fight back against whatever was killing her on the inside.

That's what Da always says, thought Kace as he crossed the cobbled street again. Something wicked was killing his poor mother from the inside. Something inside of her brain. He had found this confusing, though. If something evil was inside of her brain, why could the town's doctor not just cut it out of her?

He had asked his Da this one day, but the carpenter had only huffed and returned to the chair he was halfway through.

'It doesn't work like that,' he had said, the sawdust in his throat making him sound broken.

'Why not?' Kace asked.

'Some illnesses just can't be *cut out.*' Sander said.

Kace had always known his mother to be sick. In a drunken rant one night, his father had told him that his mother had been sick since *the day that mutt took your brother.*

This is as close as Kace had come to knowing what happened that day in their old house. In their old life. He knew it was bad and that the townspeople often gave him funny looks.

Most shook his parent's hands vigorously, saying lovely words, but a few of the long haired hippie folk said words he knew to be bad words and spat balls of thick foamy liquid in their direction.

Kace had once tried to ask why some people did this.

'We made the king do something to the dogs,' his father had said cryptically, drinking from his tankard of ale — as he did most nights.

'He's not old enough,' Brithe snapped at her husband from the other side of the dinner table.

'*The* king?!' Kace had asked, shocked, 'You know the king?'

They didn't say anything more. Instead, Brithe had stood and taken her plate into her bedroom. Sander stabbed at his rabbit stew.

'You don't need to know right now,' he said.

Kace wasn't too sure *when* he needed to know. But he patiently waited for that day to come.

Most mornings, he'd wake, and the first thing he'd do is clean his ears. Just in case that was the day he needed to know. He couldn't risk his ears being blocked and not hearing. He felt awful childish for thinking that, but still, he cleaned his ears every morning. A habit can be a hard thing to break, he found. No matter how childish.

'Bread, Ma,' Kace said, opening the thin wooden door to his parent's room. She was sitting up and looked well. A smile spread like an infection from Kace's mouth to hers.

'Would you care for some butter and jam?' he asked, knowing she would.

'Yes, please,' Brithe said, making room for her son to climb up onto the bed beside her, 'has your Da gone to work?'

'Yes, he left awfully early.'

'And you've already been across the road?' Brithe said, marvelling at the still-warm bread loaf, the little ceramic bowl of bright yellow butter and the jelly-like jam to the side.

She took the wooden chopping board from him and, with what little strength she could muster, cut herself a slice.

'I've already had mine,' Kace said proudly, 'I had a slice with fruit inside it.'

'Is that so?' Brithe said weakly.

'I was thinking,' Kace began as he opened the shutters, 'we're to run out of milk by this evening. Perchance, I could walk out to the farm to get some?'

Brithe's face was ash grey when he turned to look at her.

'You can go when your Da gets home,' she said, her face wrinkling at the sudden light.

'I can go by myself, Ma' Kace said, trying not to plead.

'Don't you have Zanty coming over?'

'It's Saturday, Ma. There's no school today.'

'Oh,' is all she could say.

'Ma, I will be home well before it's dark, and I'll take the main streets only.'

She placed her bread slice down as if her appetite had left her alone. She thought a moment, then spoke.

'There's a penny downstairs,' she said numbly.

A penny is the cost of a pint of milk, Kace thought.

'Thank you, Mother. I'll be home before you can cut your second slice.' He hugged her and bounded for the door.

'Don't tell your Da, okay?' she called after the boy.

And Kace promised that he wouldn't.

Down the wooden stairs and out onto the cobbled street he went, the penny in his pocket.

The farm was where all of Ellon got their milk.

The wealthy sent their servants, while the poor walked the short walk up the hill.

Kace meandered along the main street, past the church and the harbour and climbed the steep hill away from the crashing waves.

Just under a mile out of the town, at the top of the hill, sat the farm. A cottage, with an always half-open stable door, waited for him and his penny.

'Pint of milk, please,' Kace said politely, offering the penny.

The farmer's daughter sat on a small wooden stool inside the thatched cottage. She walked to the stable door and asked where his mother was.

'She's awful sick today,' he answered, pained at the memory of her pale face in the harsh morning sunlight. A happy yellow that bounced from her unhappily.

'Sad that,' said the farmer's daughter, taking the boy's penny and pocketing it in her overalls.

Kace felt the blood rush straight to his cheeks as the milkmaid touched his hand. No girls were ever allowed to play with him and the baker's son. They had cooties. But here, he found himself more and more intrigued by this woman. He would visit more frequently, like a timid shrew being fed, stepping closer to her. Then staying a little longer when he learnt that he wasn't going to be eaten by her. Even if she was a girl.

They'd always been a mystery to him - girls.

He'd never played with any, so he didn't know how to act around them. Their entire everything was a bit scary to him.

Even now, at the mature age of twelve, he found his palms were sweaty and his heart pumped. He tried to take a breath: you're acting like a baby, Kace. Speak to the girl.

'Do you like milk?' he asked.

'Well, of course. I am the farmer's daughter.' She snorted, making the blood rush faster. Flushing him a rosy red.

Of course, she likes milk, how silly to ask. A real man wouldn't ask something so stupid.

He knew he'd never marry the milkmaid. She was, like all beautiful people in the town of Ellon, spoken for. She was due to marry one of the king's guards. A young promising military man with a prosperous career ahead. It would be a high-profile wedding in the town's church at the end of winter, and rumour had it that the king himself would be present, making it the first time he'd visited Ellon since the decree to kill the dogs. What interest would she have in a boy like Kace? Simply a carpenter's son.

'A pint of milk for the boy,' she said, handing over the glass bottle.

He took it and immediately offered her some back. 'Because you like milk.'

She laughed and told him to scurry off. He did.

As he walked away from the cottage and back to the

town, he saw a little yard cat sitting on a bale of hay, watching him.

Looking back to ensure the milkmaid was out of sight, he walked towards the small black cat, its pupils, like little black slits, not so much as blinking. He poured the smallest amount of milk onto the stoned floor and stepped away. He looked at the bottle, ensuring that his mother would not notice the discrepancy.

He watched the baby black cat licking the creamy white liquid from the floor in two swift motions. Its little pink tongue stabbed at it ferociously. The black slit pupils looking up to either say thank you or telling him to leave.

Kace had promised not to go off the main track, but his feet took him the long way back to the town.

He carried on along the ridge towards the *forbidden house*. A house so empty and unspoken about that it could only be a source of great wonder for a little boy.

There was only one place where it was possible to see the house itself. A clearing in the trees by the tall, rusted gates revealed the house's chimneys and the edge of a turret with one broken window.

Some of the children of Ellon would claim they'd been inside the house. But nobody could describe its inside. They'd feign the dark was too thick. Or that the house had sucked the memories from them as they left.

Kace knew of only one child that could describe inside the forbidden house. The story goes that he was playing by the boundary to the house, his ball had gone over the high stone wall. When he finally made his way back down to the town, his clothes were torn, and he had a bright red fleshy wound on his thigh. After a decline in hospital, he died slowly and painfully.

Nobody knew his name, but every child knew his story. Kace had wanted to ask if he *really* existed but thought better of it.

Whenever he'd asked his parents about the boy and the story, they'd gone quiet and told him that the house was cursed.

'Death occurs there,' Sander had warned, 'stay away from that house, you hear me?'

Kace slowed his walk by the locked, rusted gate. Curiosity made him peek through the trees. As all children and adults did when passing this strange place. Not that many passed it anymore. The path to it had become overgrown, and the people that once lived there were long forgotten.

He could only see what he'd seen countless times. Chimney, turret, and a broken window.

He carried on back down the hill and towards the town. He ducked as he passed the small wooden shed where his father worked all those long hours. He heard the saw at work, a sound so synonymous with Sander. A sound from Kace's childhood, just like the repetitive gnawing of the blade, the satisfying *thunk* of the wood splitting and falling to the floor.

He passed a field where some teenagers were playing a game of Crossball. Kace could never see the appeal of the region's most popular sport. It was fierce and required little more than pure strength, in his opinion. Although, he realised he might be biased as he's never *actually* played it. None of the boys had ever invited him to the playing fields.

He continued on. Along the harbour wall to their cobbled street and up the wooden stairs.

When he entered Brithe's bedroom, he found her asleep again. He closed the door as quietly as possible and set the pint of milk on the table for tea.

He poured himself a cup of water from the brown steel jug, drinking it as if he'd never had water before, and he felt the tiredness from his walk shake off him.

Saturday was already halfway done, so he took his book and sat on the windowsill in his loft bedroom, looking out at the fishing boats bobbing just outside of the harbour.

Below him, on the cobbled street, the baker's son was drinking lemonade in the afternoon sun. A few of the town folk wandered aimlessly from shop to shop.

The distant sound of a horse and its hoofs sent him off into a reverie. He imagined riding through a forest, carefree, and racing to a princess's castle. Slaying evil and conquering good. Perhaps it was just the novel he was reading that had seeped into his consciousness. Perhaps it was the boredom of this Saturday being like any other. Or maybe he was just growing up. Maybe the bedroom he had grown up in was starting to feel all too small for him now. He picked up a pen and started to write a list of what he wanted to do before becoming *an old man.*

Shortly after dark, his father returned, and the family sat down for their supper. Not a grand affair by any means, but it was food at least. They ate fish with potatoes and carrots.

Sander had a bottle of ale he had brought home from work, whereas Brithe and Kace had lemonade. Like most suppers, the family didn't speak after the brief interaction about their day; a quick recap followed by silence.

Kace didn't like to lie to his father, but he had made a promise to his mother. And they are the most sacred of all.

'I read my book inside all day,' he said when the conversation turned to his day.

Sander grunted approvingly while Brithe stabbed at a butter-covered carrot.

'Did you have homework from Zanty?'

'No,' Kace lied. The two parents exchanged a look that told him they didn't believe him.

'I'll do it before Monday morning,' he pleaded.

They said nothing, but the carpenter's silence spoke of his disproval. He drank from his bottle of ale and said nothing more for the evening.

Kace wanted to be anywhere but those quiet family suppers, he wanted freedom beyond freedom.

He felt like, below the table, thick metal chains were weighing him to the ground. Like a ship that wanted to sail, but dragged an anchor along the seabed.

But, it's funny, he would come to miss those quiet family suppers. When everything fell apart, those memories were heavenly.

2.

His parents had always told him to be grateful that he had one of the best educations in the whole of Ellon.

Total dedication to her one student.

Exclusivity.

No bullies or distractions.

Kace had heard it all repeatedly but still didn't see the benefit himself. He longed for the classroom anecdotes the baker's son told him. How once, during a lesson on plants, their teacher had gotten an allergic reaction to a particularly potent Watercrumb and had to be doused in cane sugar syrup to stop him from ballooning into a full-blown circle.

'His hands were the size of Crossballs!' Wyeth had recounted, making Kace choke on his bread roll at the thought.

Zanty had taught him since he was five years old. Every morning she'd arrive in the same black, draping, cloth top. Kace had never seen her wear any other top. Was it the same one, or did she have many identical ones?

Kace would sometimes sniff her on a Friday to see if it smelt like it had been worn for five days. But she always smelt of the same vanilla essence mixed with honey.

She drank tea all day but never used the toilets. Kace thought she must have a bladder the size of water tank.

She was predictable. Kace was bored of her and everything she had to say.

'I once knew someone who had a bad reaction to Watercrumb,' he said, trying to inspire a conversation and invoke the image of that circle teacher.

'Sugar,' Zanty said dismissively. 'That's the antidote to Watercrumb. Especially cane sugar syrup. Write that down.'

So he did. In his little notebook of plants, he wrote that cane sugar syrup is the antidote to a Watercrumb reaction. Not nearly as fun as learning in a class of his peers as a teacher poured syrup over his colleague.

After lunch on a particularly boring Monday, they did basic equations, and Zanty set the homework. Which was just *work* for Kace. Because all school work he did was at home.

Zanty finished the end of her tea, picked up the lemon wedge from the drained cup, and sucked it dry and stringy. As she always did.

She left, and Kace started to do the housework. He cleaned all of the windows, swept the floors, and took the bed sheets off of the strings that hung from window to window. He longed for a garden, but instead, their sheets flapped like flags from their second-story windows.

Evening came, and Brithe said she was too unwell to get out of bed and cook. So Kace began to make one of the only things he could make properly: soup.

He smiled as he dropped a leaf of Watercrumb into it, imagining Circle Man.

The soup was more of a broth. It was a clear liquid with small floating vegetables, chunks of stringy meat and green leaves. Salt and pepper brought it together.

He lay the table for two, with a homemade wooden board holding the end of Saturday's bread, two bowls, two spoons and some butter.

He brought Brithe's supper into her, waking her up and ensuring she took at least two spoonfuls before he left the room.

When he returned to the dining table, Sander had come back, kicking off his big black boots at the door.

'Where's your mother?' he asked as if she'd be anywhere but in her bed.

'She's feeling too poorly to eat with us,' Kace said, pouring out two soup bowls.

'But she made this, at least?' Sander asked, opening an ale and using it to point at the soup. Kace nodded. He doesn't know why, but he thought his father would be more pleased with the thought of her having made it. He had once heard Wyeth say that a person's brain can feed their tastebuds different stories based on who they thought had made the bread. He imagined the same was with soup. Brithe was a good cook; if he thought she'd made it, perhaps he'd enjoy it more. He wanted his father to enjoy the food so very much.

'It's good,' the man said, sipping from the soup and the ale in turns.

Kace nodded and drank from his bowl. It was the smallest of all three bowls. He was used to this. He was only little, after all. And his father needed the biggest portion as he worked the hardest, then his mother, who needed to fight her illness. Last and certainly least was Kace's portion. Small, but enough for him. His father often recounted a story about a pack of dogs that hadn't enough food, so they ate the smallest in the pack, and then the next smallest, and then the next. Until there was just one dog in the pack left. And it died of starvation.

Kace had barely been seven when he first heard that story, but three things stuck with him: one, he would be the first to be eaten in his family pack. Two, was it really true? And three, if it *was* true, surely humans and dogs weren't too different.

The shrill scream woke most of Ellon up. It was dark, and an angry wind carried the scream down the cobbled streets of the town like a rampant virus.

Sander was one of the many men who ran onto the street to investigate.

The woman kneeled in the doorway of the town hall, desperately banging on the door. The sheriff finally stepped out to the distressed woman.

A crowd of sleepy, adrenaline-fueled townspeople circled the scene like it were a busker about to perform the best of songs.

'Help me!' the woman cried, her green eyes full of fear, 'There is a mutt by the market square. A vicious thing.' She was crying now. Tears cascaded like she'd just run from death itself. She was at least drunk, if not on drugs.

The crowd murmured concerns, the more decisive of them returning home to retrieve their weapon of choice.

'We must find the mutt and kill him!' a voice shouted.

The sheriff turned to the mob of townspeople and

told them to go back to bed. 'We will deal with the dog,' he said.

Kace had just joined the crowd and took Sander's big, rough hand in his. His father looked angry at seeing him out of bed but angrier at the thought of a dog roaming the town.

The sheriff stepped forward and, with snake-like eyes, looked coldly at the woman.

'And what were you doing in the market square at this hour?'

The crowd fell silent as the reality of whom she was dawned on them all.

'Taking a walk,' the woman said weakly.

The sheriff turned to the mob. 'I urge you all to go home, please.' And then he took the woman by the arm and dragged her up from her knees.

'I was just trying to protect the young ones! The town!' the woman pleaded helplessly. Her accent was not native to Ellon. And the crowd whispered this.

Dirty outsider.

'Please,' she begged, 'I have a daughter!'

Kace watched as the crowd went from an irate mob to an audience of a spectacle. The sheriff dragged the woman off towards the back of the town hall, a place that Kace would come to know well: the town's jail cell.

The crowd began to disperse as the sheriff's men barked orders to go to the market square at once.

Kace and Sander walked slowly back along the cobbled street to the house.

'Who was she?' the boy asked.

'A whore,' he said, spitting a ball of phlegm perfectly between two cobbled stones.

When Kace got back into his bed, he heard the sound of a shotgun being loaded and the door closing. He looked out of his window and down at the darkening figure of his father walking towards the market square.

The following morning, while bringing Brithe her breakfast, Kace told the night's story. She was very pale these days, so he couldn't tell if she grew paler. But he thought she might have.

'What will happen to the dog?' Kace asked.

'Nothin' good,' his mother gravely replied.

'What about the woman?'

'Nothin' good either.'

The afternoon sun was just setting over the market square when Kace pushed his way through the dense crowd. He thought that perhaps a musician might be performing in the centre circle as they so often did. But when he got through, he saw no musician but instead two shapes hanging from thick brown rope.

The first was small and furry. A thing with white teeth, triangle ears, a long tail, and the saddest eyes Kace had ever seen.

While the second was the woman who had told the town about the first.

It hadn't been the first time that Kace had seen death in the Market Square. Each time it felt more harrowing, though. Death never got any easier.

He looked at the bodies in wonder, the townspeople

had always told him that dogs were not like humans in any way, but here, hanging from the beam. He couldn't see how they'd treated the woman and the dog any differently.

The 'whore and the mutt' was all Ellon talked about in those days after. It divided opinion. But the overall message was, 'Well, what's one less mutt and one less whore?'

In the market square, the vicar prayed for the woman's soul, asking God for forgiveness on her behalf. Which Kace thought was odd, surely forgiveness can only be given by God if the one who sinned is asking?

People gawked at the two lifeless bodies for days after.

But finally, after five sunsets, the sheriff's men cut them down and took them to be buried in a hole near the church. Not quite a grave, as such. But a place to cover them and allow the town never to speak of them again. And just three days after the soil had flattened, the gossiping stopped, and the town forgot about them.

Wooden stairs, cobble street, across the road to the baker's son. Kace did his familiar route, taking the freshest loaf in the basket.

'Would you like to play Crossball with us later?' Wyeth asked.

'I'm not very good at it,' Kace admitted. The baker's son shrugged, telling him it didn't matter.

'I'll ask my parents,' he said, before going back across the cobbled street, up the wooden stairs and into the house.

'But it's dangerous,' Sander pleaded to neither Brithe nor Kace specifically.

'If he wants to play, let him,' Brithe said weakly.

'I'll walk with Wyeth,' Kace pleaded. He wanted to be a normal boy and play sports with friends his age. Why was that so hard to get?

Finally, his father gave in. He watched Kace leave, cross the street, and meet Wyeth outside the bakery. The boys waved and walked towards the playing fields.

'Why are your parents so paranoid?' Wyeth asked as Kace kicked a pebble along the road mindlessly.

He shrugged.
'They're just scared of things. Scared of all the things they know about that I don't.'

'Oh.'

'Parents know everything.'

'Nu-uh, my Da got the amount of salt in his twisty bread rolls wrong for years, didn't he?' It was Wyeth's turn to kick the pebble now. 'I accidentally put too much in one day, and they came out well better.'

'Oh.'

'So, yeah, sometimes parents aren't always right.' He kicked the pebble, making it skim towards the sheriff's horse. It bounced off of its hoof, startling the tall horse.

'Oi!' shouted the mounted sheriff and the boys ran until their legs were sore and the sheriff was long out of sight.

At the playing fields, Kace felt suddenly nervous at the prospect of playing Crossball. It had been a good idea in principle, but to see the crowds of sweaty Ellon boys all running and tackling each other made him long to be anywhere but there.

'Come on then,' Wyeth said, still panting from the run and dragging Kace towards a group of boys that were far too tall and far too fast for Kace to feel like he had a chance.

The first boy who ran into Kace knocked him so hard that his vision blurred before he even hit the grass.

'Get up, tiny!' one of his teammates barked at him. Not exactly teamwork, that.

A second boy, moments later, also sent Kace's vision askew.

He had been there for an entire eight minutes when he decided to simply run away.

'Kace!' Wyeth called, but all of the boys were laughing now so he didn't run after his friend. Kace ran up the hill and into the forest surrounding the playing fields.

He ran until the boys' cruel laughs petered out, and the forest's silence screamed at him instead.

A small bird perched on a branch and, through the quiet, its chirp was as clear as if it had been inside of Kace's head. He stared at its white chest and dusty brown feathers. The bird's tiny marble eyes told Kace where to go. He walked deeper into the forest, each step feeling like he was moving away from bad and towards good. Whatever that meant.

The faraway weak cries of the playing fields became null. His best friend substituted for a new one: the silence.

He found a fallen down tree. It bridged over a small ditch.

Climb me, the tree begged. And he did.

It was sturdier than he had anticipated, its strength was comforting. He sat in the middle of it, as if to stop it from tipping in one direction or another. Like, if he remained parallel, then nature wouldn't notice his intrusion.

He sat and took small breaths, noticing the rise and fall of his chest for the first time. He didn't know one could hear their heartbeat in their ear until that first day in the forest.

He closed his eyes and breathed deep and slow until a tranquil state made it all too natural.

His eyes snapped open at a singular sound: a rustle of some kind. A slow rustle.

From behind a thick bush, the figure stepped out. Kace expected a person. Something taller. But his eyes had to drop to the shadow of a small furry creature. Its triangle ears and its trepidatious tail.

He stopped breathing momentarily as the creature stood before him, as shocked as the boy. He didn't know whether to run, hide or kill it. Neither boy nor dog.

So they just stood staring at each other, like two dumb statues.

The white-chested bird landed between them like a Crossball referee… Its chirp made both boy and dog look at it. The small movements of their heads were just a peace offering. *I'll look away if you promise not to attack.*

When Kace looked back at the dog, it moved as if

readying itself.

This is how I will die, Kace thought.

But no such death came to boy or dog. Instead, with each of its four legs, it stepped back gently and, in a flash, was gone.

Kace felt his heartbeat slow again. The rhythm in his ears returned to a slower state.

He jumped from the fallen tree and jogged out of the forest.

The walk home was long, and his feet were bleeding by the time he was climbing the wooden stairs and his calves ached for a bath. The warm water softened and relieved the tightness. He thought about the dog in the forest. Why didn't it attack? Did it look scared, or was it completely stoic? Kace couldn't tell.

If that is as scary as they get, it's not the worst, he thought.

'Kace!' Sander's booming voice shouted.

Kace, naked and fearful, jumped from the bath and grabbed a long t-shirt for his modesty. At first, he thought that somehow his father had read his mind and knew he was thinking about dogs. He panicked at the thought, but the next shout was not angry. It was a sad shout.

'Kace,' he said, 'get the doctor. Please, it's your Ma.'

Kace ran out to the voice. His father stood shaking Brithe, shouting for Kace to run for the doctor.

He ran as fast as he could, not caring that his long shirt barely covered him.

The boys returning from the playing fields laughed and tried to trip him up.

Kace banged on the surgery door and begged the doctor to come and help.

But by the time they'd made it back along the cobble street and up the wooden stairs, Brithe had died. Her body, cold and rigid, lay atop the bedsheets.

The doctor dropped a mysterious medicine into her lifeless mouth, but his efforts were fruitless.

Her illness had finally caught up to her.

A bottle lay broken by the bedside table. A bottle of thick, gloopy medicine once prescribed to help her. The bottle was empty now, which Kace found odd.

He could have sworn it was full the night previous.

The doctor covered her with a sheet, and the sheriff's men came to take her away.

The street was lined with silent people. They all stared as the body was carried towards the town hall. Kace and his father followed it in procession.

A drunk stumbled into its path, making a mounted guard bark at him to move. The whole town fell quiet. The way it did when a respectable person died. The silence brought comfort to Kace. The respect was like a soft feather bed on this turbulent plummet. He wanted to shake his mother until she woke.

Oh, dear, I was only having a deep sleep!

And the town would laugh endlessly. His mother would be alive and talking to him once again. He could smell the perfume she doused herself in every morning. Even on the days when she was too sick to get up, she'd smell the same floral smell. It was like ginger mixed with pepper. Or tulips and spice. It had a unique smell that was hers.

But he wasn't alive to wake and spray it. The last time he'd ever get the aroma was that morning she died. Before she'd taken too many of her pills, she'd opened the perfume bottle and covered the room in it. Even on her final day, she ensured the smell lingered in the air.

Kace cried hard at the thought of her scent fading into nothingness. Taking her with it.

The sheriff's men brought the body into the town hall. A dignified place to store her until her final place of rest.

It was spring, and Kace thought about what a poor time it was to die. The irony of burying the dead in soil that was beginning to grow new life.

'Perhaps it's the circle of life,' Wyeth had said to make him feel better.

'It feels more like being mocked,' Kace said.

Kace never saw his mother's body again. Days later, when her body exited the town hall, it was locked away in a thick wooden box, handmade by Sander himself. As it passed him, he could swear he smelt the last of her perfume. But perhaps he only wanted to. Either way, if it was there or not, it didn't matter. He smelt it, regardless.

The coffin was taken to a plot of land in the church and covered in soil.

They drank ale and wine in the town hall afterwards. The wake crowd milled around, paying their respects. Sander stood by the doors to the town hall until darkness came and the last of the condolences had been said.

When he returned home, Kace had made supper.

'Tastes just like your mother's,' Sander said, drinking the soup.

3.

Sander had always loved an ale. But Kace watched as his father's drinking increased dramatically after Brithe's death. He'd have a few bottles at home before bed, but now his drinking was taking him from the house. He was spending more time at the local tavern than ever before. Kace wondered if the only thing that made him come home was his wife. And if he was even good enough.

The Oak was aptly named due to the tall oak tree that grew outside of it. It was the best tavern in Ellon after The Hairy Hound got burnt down for affiliating itself with dogs. Not that it was, it had only been poorly named so.

Kace had been sitting in his room reading when his father knocked and asked him to join him at the tavern. For the boy, this felt like a right of passage, of some kind.

'A pint of ale for me and a lemonade for the boy,' Sander declared to the barmaid, fishing in his carpenter's overalls for coins.

'One and a half pennies,' she said, pulling a pint from one of the tavern's taps.

'Sod it,' Sander said, 'same for the boy. Two ales.'

'But Da,' Kace started, like he'd forgotten he was only twelve.

'That small boy don't look fourteen yet,' said the barmaid.

'Aye, but he pays two pennies for an ale, you know.'

The barmaid squinted at the baby-faced boy.

'Perhaps he do be fourteen,' she said, producing

another tankard from beneath the counter.

Sander paid three pennies, two for the tavern, one for the barmaid, and they sat on a table by the fire. Kace had never tasted ale before and couldn't help but retch at his first sip.

'It'll put hairs on your chest, this,' Sander said, taking two large mouthfuls without so much as flinching.

He watched his father in wonder; how was that even possible?

'To your Ma,' he said, offering his tankard across the table.

Clink.

'Da?' Kace asked after braving another sip. 'Does an afterlife exist?'

'I sure hope not,' he grimaced.

'Why not?'

'Your Ma will be awful lonely up there, won't she?'

Kace thought about this, then asked. 'But won't she be with my brother?'

Sander looked over his tankard like he saw his son for the first time.

'Maybe,' he started but shook away whatever he was thinking quickly, 'your brother was too young to get into an afterlife. You need to be accepted into the church.'

'Am I accepted into the church?' Kace asked.

'No.'

'But what if I die tomorrow?' he asked, the ale making him dizzy.

Sander shrugged, 'Didn't do your Ma much good, did it?'

They didn't say much more that evening. Both man and boy taking respectively large and small sips until Sander's fourth tankard was empty, and Kace's first was too.

Lying in his low bed in the house that was once a home, Kace watched the beam above him spin in a silly way. He felt a laugh coming from nothing in particular. He felt like someone had deflated a balloon of stress over his head. He drifted softly into sleep and had the most vivid dream of his mother's homemade pie that made him cry gently upon awaking.

The morning came, bringing the worst of headaches with it. A hammer and nail in his temple.

Kace had forgotten to close his shutters, so the early morning sun stabbed at him painfully. His mouth was dry and tasted rank. He went immediately to the bucket of water by the door and washed his mouth clean. How could a man drink more than one of those ales if this is how bad it felt afterwards?

Suddenly he understood why his father would often wake and immediately drink another. Perhaps the constant drinking kept this feeling at bay? He figured it was worth trying.

He went to the empty kitchen, for his father had already left for work and opened a bottle of Oatmeal Stout. Again the taste was vile but, not too long after, the worst subsided and he felt giddy. His lessons would be much better if he felt like this.

He finished the Stout and hid the empty bottle in his father's sock drawer. Surely he wouldn't notice one more getting added to his collection?

He'd first found his father's collection a while back, asking Brithe why he had such, had brought a blank expression to her face and she told him that was his *Da's medication.*

That drunk morning, when Zanty and her draping, black top arrived, the boy was half-cut and giddy.

'Why do you always wear the same top,' he bravely asked. Her wavy sleeves were swaying even more so in his drunken state. The tutor looked taken aback.

'What business is that to you, young man?'

'Do you wash the same one every night?'

Zanty stood. 'It is my teaching uniform. Have you been drinking?'

He tried to contain his burp, but burped anyway. His eyes were hazy too, the picture of a young drunk. 'No, miss.'

'Wait until your father hears about this.'

'He'll congratulate me,' the boy slurred.

'Well, then, your mother!' Despite being drunk, he saw the moment she realised her error and started to fuss about needing to go to the toilet.

'But you've never once urinated inside this house?' the boy said cheekily as she tried to make her exit. 'I bet you don't even know where it is.'

She didn't. So instead, she locked herself in the front room and prayed to God that this drunk devil child be disciplined.

Drunkenly, Kace left the house and the praying woman, and he wandered the cobbled street towards

The Oak tavern. But without his father, the barmaid would not serve him. He thought of calling by his father at work, but he imagined this was the quickest way to getting locked away in his room.

He went to where the young boys and girls of Ellon would drink in secret: the playing fields. Alas, it was a school day, and he found them empty. So, he wandered the route he had just recently taken, up the verge and into the forest behind the fields.

He wanted the tree again.

It had taken him a lot longer to find it, but finally, there, like a cylinder bridge, it lay.

Kace climbed onto it and, on hands and knees, made it to the centre. He sat a long while as the Oatmeal Stout calmed itself in his stomach, levelling him off again.

Would Zanty call into the workshop? Would he be in a lot of trouble when he went home?

He figured. So he stayed for as long as he could.

Watching the birds flitter in and out of the tree tops, the sun's journey across the sky, and finally when he could no longer avoid it, he started the trek home.

One of the strangest sensations is the feeling of being watched.

It's like an itch that can't be scratched. A longing to turn and see eyes.

But when Kace turned, he couldn't see any eyes. But he was sure he was being watched. As sure as he's ever been about anything.

Surely enough, Sander was furious. When Kace returned home, it was clear that the ale cupboard had been well raided by his father.

'Where the bloody hell were you?' he spat towards the little boy. 'Running off from Zanty like that, you little git!'

'I'm sorry,' the small boy said in a small voice.

'She's gone off to pray for you at the church. Says the devil himself is inside of you. What if the vicar hears her? You'll never get accepted into the church!'

'I just felt sick after the ale last night, so I had one more.'

'Ale does that to a man. If you can't handle it, you clearly aren't one.'

'I am a man,' said Kace defiantly.

'No, you're just a little baby boy who can't stomach one ale.'

The crash of the glass bottle made both man and boy jump. The ale waterfalled off the table's edge, prompting Sander into a flustered cleaning state. In the chaos, Kace slipped off so as not to be seen crying.

Men don't cry. Especially men of Ellon, his father had told him plenty.

By the time he had gotten to his bedroom, his eyes were hot and wet.

He lay face down in the sheets, wrapping himself tightly, and allowed himself to cry.

It was the first time he'd cried since his mother had died, and it felt cleansing. He felt washed when he emerged from the tangled bedsheets.

Below him, his father was scraping a pot. Supper, he hoped. He realised how hungry he was all of a sudden.

As Kace rinsed his clothes in the bucket, the sound of a bowl was placed by his bedroom door.

'Supper,' said Sander through the door before returning back downstairs, his thick boots plodding along the landing, loudly.

Kace opened the door and picked up the bowl of stew.

It was far too salty for his liking, but he ate the entire bowl quickly. He heard his father leave for the tavern shortly after.

He watched the hunched dark figure walking down the street. He doubted he'd ever be invited to the tavern with his father again.

He picked up a new novel and tumbled into its story.

He finished the book in one sitting and didn't remember falling asleep. He lifted the hardback from his face, like he'd used it as an eyeshade. He laughed gently to himself and set the book aside.

The morning sun was non-existent that morning. In fact, if it wasn't for the church bells, he would have thought it was still night.

It was grey, and the rain sounded sad on his bedroom window. Like it was willingly stepping off of the cloud and plummeting to the surface below.

He washed his face and went down to the kitchen. It was empty but instead of opening a stout, he cut a thin slice of bread, to leave a generous helping for Sander, and made himself breakfast. He wondered what time his father would awake. He found it odd that his big steel-toe boots sat at the door still. Was he not meant to be at his workshop?

Kace ate his buttered bread and, when the lack of noise from the room above alarmed him too much, he went to wake Sander.

'Da?' he said into the dark room. His father's body looked so very small in the bed he used to share. He breathed slowly and peacefully. Kace couldn't bring himself to wake him. He hadn't seen his face so calm in a long while. Silently, he closed the door and left the man to sleep.

Zanty didn't come that morning, which was of no shock to Kace.

She probably thought less of him. He wondered if Sander would find a new tutor or if his education days were over.

He wanted to ask if he could enrol in the local big school, but thought it best to wait until this storm passed. Except it was only the beginning.

When Sander woke, he stormed down into the kitchen, swearing under his breath.

'Why didn't you wake me, boy?!' he hissed, pulling his big boots on.

'You looked like you needed the rest.'

'What I need,' said his father, 'is to earn enough coin to keep you alive!'

And, with a bang of the door, he was out to his workshop. He didn't so much as notice Zanty was not sitting in her usual spot, drinking her first of many teas.

Staring down the barrel of a full day to himself, Kace felt overwhelmingly lonely. He crossed to the bakery but, of course, Wyeth was at school.

'No lessons today?' the baker quizzed when he entered the doughy room.

'Nu-uh, Zanty is sick,' he said, picking up a fresh loaf.

'Is that so?'

'Do you not believe me?'

'I do, of course, young Kace. I just know how you boys are.'

He smiled innocently and asked the baker to put the loaf onto his family's ledger.

'No coin today?' the fat, bearded baker asked.

'Sorry, Da isn't good at giving me coins. But you know he'll stop by to pay it off.'

'Aye, well, I know where ye live.'

Kace bit into the loaf, ravenous suddenly, the crumbs flaking to the shop floor.

'Hm. You really are a master baker,' Kace said, making the man fluster for some reason.

'Get out of here with that, will you? You're making this look like a kitchen for the poor. Use a plate, boy,' the baker smiled, shoeing him back out to the cobbled street.

But Kace didn't return home. Instead, he walked out to the forest.

He sat on the fallen tree and ate the fresh bread in a state of calm. The house felt like it had no air in it. Like he was suffocating inside those rooms. But here, he felt the air fill his lungs to a size he didn't know possible.

The crack of a branch didn't seem odd at first. Maybe because it was a common noise with birds building nests, or perhaps because he hoped he'd see what he saw.

He recognised the triangle ears at first.

Slowly, he hid the bread behind his back. But he knew the dog would know he had food. *Those hounds have such cruel noses, they can smell it all,* he had heard his father say. Yet still, he hid it. An attempt to conceal the bait.

The creature stepped towards the boy, making his heart rate increase by two with each step those hairy paws took.

Kace had a thought. He took his hand out from behind his back, broke a piece off and threw it as far as he could. The creature did not run to it. Its wide eyes watched it fly but quickly looked back at him as if to ask why he'd just thrown away perfectly good food.

The boy tore another piece of bread and ate it gloatingly, gaining confidence he suddenly thought might get him killed.

'Nah-nah,' he teased, 'I have food, and you don't.'

The creature cocked its head like it was trying desperately to understand what the boy had said.

'Eat me,' Kace pleaded. 'Take me away from this town!'

He began to rub the bread on him, dusting himself in crumbs. The creature stepped forward.

The dog was only a metre or so away. He froze as if the grim reaper himself was standing in front of him.

Kace slowly extended the rest of the bread out to the creature.

Sniff, sniff.

The boy's hand shook, so the little creature took the bread as gently as possible.

Like it knew not to be too quick.

With a bite of bread, it darted back into the bushes. Kace watched as it scurried out of sight, and he sat still, waiting for nothing in particular, before standing and walking home.

4.

It was six days later when the baker's ledger finally caught up to Kace.

On his morning walk to work, Sander met the baker who asked if he would drop in the penny before evening.

'But we have no outstanding debts,' said Sander, confused.

'Young Kace stopped in just shy of a week ago,' the baker replied.

A confused Sander pondered this all day, racking his brain. Finally, when he got home and found the boy in his usual reading spot, he confronted him.

'Did you buy and eat an entire loaf of bread?'

Kace's eyes darted to the floor, looking for the answer there, perhaps.

'Um,' he started, but Sander cut him off before he could say anything more.

'The baker said we owe him a penny.'

'Yes,' the boy admitted, 'I bought the bread and ate it all.'

'Kace,' his father said disappointedly, 'were you expecting me to pay it off for you? That is not how I raised you.'

'You hardly raised me,' Kace found himself saying.

'Don't you talk back at me,' His father stepped into the room, a fat thud with each step,
'I will not be paying for this loaf. I shall walk across to the baker and tell him to put the debt in *your* name.'

'But I have no way to make coin,' Kace pleaded.

'Perhaps you should have thought about that before you devoured an entire loaf to yourself!'

And with that, his bedroom door slammed shut, and then the front door.

Out the window, he watched his father walk across the street to the baker. To fulfil his promise, no doubt. How was a twelve-year-old expected to make money?

He walked up to the farm after the next sunrise. He leant into the stable door and asked the milkmaid if he could help.

'I'll do a day of work for just a penny,' he said.

'I don't reckon ye know a cow from a goat, kid.' She smirked.

'Nay, I do and all. Cows are big fat things; goats are small and horny.'

'Is that so?' The milkmaid laughed, tossing a bucket of water into the drain. Kace wasn't too sure why she was laughing, but he let her. Her laugh was sweet.

'I can mind the cottage for you. A day off would be nice?' He pressed.

'I take two days off, kid. My wedding and the day after my wedding. Otherwise, work carries on.'

Perhaps she took pity on him, for the next thing she said made his day feel like a hot summer's day.

'There's a house on the other side of the harbour. Lady Viaol. Her milk boy is in bed with an illness. Maybe she wants a new little boy to fetch their milk every morning?'

'Lady Viaol,' Kace marvelled, 'Would you put in a word for me?'

'I don't know you, kid, and my word is worth more than your penny.'

So, he walked to the house himself, following her detailed instructions.

Past the harbour, up the slip road, right at the blossom tree, behind the royal blue gate.

He stood in front of it, unsure of how he might get the attention of its residents. He tried the gate, but it was locked. Disheartened, he sat at one of the grand pillars awaiting some sort of movement.

After what felt like an eternity, a stable door by the side of the house opened, and a prim and proper lady came out on the back of the whitest horse he'd ever seen.

She matched the horse. She was as white as snow, with white hair and white jodhpurs. The only flash of colour was the strikingly gold necklace of a rearing horse across her chest.

'Excuse me?' said the boy through the spokes of the gate.

'Not today,' said the woman, preparing to shoo the boy away.

'I've come to ask if you need a new milk boy,' Kace said.

'And how might one know that?'

'The milkmaid told me. She said she'd give her word to my service.' He didn't like lying to his potential employer but, like most small towns, Ellon traded on who knew who.

'We require two bottles daily, in the morning before sunrise and again before supper. My husband pays half a penny per bottle delivered. Speed is important for us.'

'I have some of the fastest legs in Ellon,' said Kace proudly. 'I have always been a wanderer.'

Again, he lied. His parents had hardly ever let him out as a child, but the many novels on his bookcase had sent his mind into all sorts of adventures, so he felt that maybe he could get away with this one. His mind often wandered, even if his body only ever stayed in the one room.

'Very well,' the lady said, 'We've had two bottles today, so we'd like the first delivery tomorrow before we wake. You can leave them with the groundsman.' She pointed towards a small wooden hut adjacent to the horse's barn.

'Thank you,' said Kace, giving a sharp bow for what reason he did not know. 'Your horse is beautiful.'

'Aye, thank you, she's racing tomorrow. I'm going to get her moving.'

'Will she win?' he asked.

'Ask the groundsman if he has a bet on her,' she quipped, kicking her legs out, commanding the horse forwards.

Walking home, he passed the playing fields and one of the only ways into the forest he knew.

He considered walking into it.

Was the dog in there waiting for him? Would it meet him if he walked into the darkness?

He shook his head and continued on back to the cobbled street.

'I got a job,' Kace said over dinner.

'Aye?' Sander said, looking up from the bleeding lamb on his plate.

'Delivering milk to Lady Viaol.'

Sander made a sound that he couldn't make out as approval or its opposite. He supposed it was the latter. Disapproval for entrepreneurship.

'A bottle before sunrise and a bottle before supper,' Kace tried to say with a proud face. Maybe his father wouldn't be so quick to shut it down if he acted confident.

'No. Kace, you are not to wander the streets in the dark.'

'But I need to repay my debt,' Kace said.

'Find a job that has you working appropriate hours.'

'There are no jobs in this town!'

'You can work with me,' his father said, with an unmistakable flicker of regret in his eyes as he did.

'I don't want to work for you,' Kace said into his plate of supper, ashamed at the truth of his statement.

He couldn't think of many things worse than spending hour after hour in his father's hot and dry workshop sawing plank after plank of wood. Bleeding and blistering, all for the sake of a chair. Sander took a relieving swig of his ale and stood. It's like there was a fire in the pit of his stomach he needed to douse in liquid.

'I suspect you are going to the tavern,' Kace said, looking out to the darkness of the night.

'And what if I am?'

'But I can't go out to work?'

'I'm a man, Kace. You can go out when you start to act like one.'

And Kace again was left alone to fall into the world of his novel.

As he drifted to sleep, one thing was evidently clear: he was going to deliver the milk to Lady Viaol.

And he did.

And his father must have suspected such defiance as, in the darkness of the morning, his father sat waiting for him. Shotgun in hand.

'Take this,' his father said, handing him the gun.

Kace nodded thanks and walked out into the blackness of the early morning..

He'd only fired a gun once in his life. Sander had taken him out to the forest, and together they stalked a deer.

'Shoot him,' his father had pressed.

Kace raised the heavy shotgun and pointed it between the oblivious deer's eyes. Stupidly, the skinny brown animal stood, unaware and chewing dewy grass in the open.

'It's an easy shot, Kace,' Sander shout-whispered.

But he had still missed. The sound of the gun startled the quick deer back into the foliage. The bullet had hit the thin tree, causing no harm to anything.

'Not even close,' Sander had spat, taking the gun from his son and turning away.

But Kace disagreed. He'd been right on a target.

As he walked to the farm, shotgun in hand, he thought of a place to hide it. What would Lady Viaol think of him turning up with a shotgun? She'd have the groundsman decorate him with his own bullet before he could even explain. A boy like Kace couldn't walk into a wealthy area carrying a shotgun. Sander should have known this. Perhaps he did, thought Kace, scared at the thought that his own father would wish him imprisoned.

He tried to find a suitable bush to hide the gun, but no such place existed. He didn't want the ugly town to be gifted a free gun. It had the habit of killing those who were vulnerable. To leave a gun out in the open felt like a sacrificial act. *Take this and kill.*

'I'm here to collect Lady Viaol's first bottle,' Kace said, 'and could I store this here?'

He pulled the shotgun up to the top half of the stable door. The milkmaid stood quickly.

'Kid! What are you doing? Put that away.'

'Sorry, my father gave it to me for protection.'

'Protection from what?'

'The dogs, I suppose.'

'Them evil things will get you before you load your gun.'

Kace thought back to the dog in the forest, at his gentle bite of the bread, and found this hard to believe.

'Well, could I keep it here until after I've dropped the milk, please?'

'Aye, but be sure to pick it up before my father returns from the sheds. Otherwise, he's claiming it as his, isn't he.'

He thanked her, exchanged the gun for milk, and started the walk back down to the town, past the harbour and up the far hill to Lady Viaol's estate.

The drop was underwhelming. It's not like he expected much, but it was as quick as anything.

At the gate, he called out to the hut, and the groundsman stepped out, walked over and took the bottle from him without a word.

'Do I get half a penny, sir?' Kace called to the white-haired man's back.

'You get the full penny when you come with the evening bottle,' he grunted.

Again, Kace called for him, 'Have you got a bet on this evening?'

The groundsman turned. 'On whom?'

'On Lady Viaol's horse? The pretty white one.'

'Who's asking,' he squinted his eyes as he asked.

'Me, sir.'

'I might have a small flutter, aye.' He slammed the hut shut and probably returned to bed.

Kace walked back to the farm, retrieved the gun from the milkmaid—who had pretended it had gone missing and made Kace's heart stop briefly—and then went home to bathe his tired feet.

Sander didn't ask how it had gone. He probably cared, but to not address it was to not think about the perils that lay in the darkness of suburban Ellon.

Zanty was persuaded to return for her lessons on the condition that Kace attended church with her in the evening.

To chase away the demons, she had said to Sander, who didn't want the trouble of finding a new tutor.

They had lessons until late afternoon, after which Kace would do his pre-supper milk run and meet Zanty at the church for service.

The vicar was particularly slow that evening. The penny's weight in the boy's pocket burnt into his thigh. He wanted desperately to pay off the baker and tell his father that he had done so.

The end of the service finally came, and he ran out, with hardly so much as a goodbye to Zanty, and raced to the baker. But it was closed. He kicked at the dirt, looking up to his dark and empty bedroom window. He knew it was wrong, but he didn't care. He walked back down the high street and into one of the less reputable gambling rooms. He felt like a proper adult, and he loved it. He sat at a high table and swung his short legs stupidly.

'Are ye here by yourself, little fella?' the barman asked.

'I'm here to put a bet on Lady Viaol's horse,' Kace said an octave or two deeper than his normal voice.

'Drink to bet. That's the rule.'

'Half an ale and half a penny on the horse,' Kace said confidently.

A man next to him looked up from his stout.

'Do you know something about that filly?' he asked quietly, as the barman went about the half pint of ale.

'I think her horses are magnificent,' Kace said back proudly.

'Five pennies on the same,' the man said to the

barman. And then turned to Kace, 'If she loses, I'll have your head on a stick.' He winked, but Kace felt it wasn't playful.

He sat drinking his half pint of ale. After what felt like an age, the door finally opened. A boy about Kace's age stood panting with a slip of paper.

'Word from the first race of the evening,' he said between breaths.

Kace and the five-penny man leant forward.

'Winner all right, Kaya.'

Kace wasn't sure of the horse's name, so he could only turn to the five-penny man for clarity.

'Aye, you're a lucky boy,' he said, smirking.

The barman nodded at them both and went to open his cash box.

Kace walked home with two pennies in his pocket. He'd drank half an ale and still managed to double his pay thanks to Lady Viaol's horse. He smiled at the thought of doing the same again the next day. Who needs to sweat in a workshop all day when one can just do a quick walk for a penny and double it on the horses? *Foolproof,* he thought.

The next morning, he was up and at the farm, then off to earn the first half of his penny.

'Tell Lady Viaol I said congratulations on the win yesterday,' he said to the groundsman, who grunted in either agreement or disagreement. It was unclear. But Kace suspected the former.

It was Saturday and Zanty wasn't due over so, with yet another free day and a penny in his pocket, he walked to the butchers, bought himself a slab of cold meat for lunch and, impulsively, a near meatless bone. He walked out to the forest, to the fallen tree he was becoming so very fond of. He sat eating his ham lunch and bathed in the peace.

He wasn't startled when the dog came this time.

It's like they'd planned to meet. Both froze for a moment as if asking permission to engage further, and when Kace gave a little nod, the dog trotted towards him and sat.

He confidently took the butcher's bone out of his satchel and threw it to the dog.

'Good catch,' he said as the dog's white teeth crunched down on the bone.

The dog looked up as if to say thank you, and the two ate their lunch in silence.

'You could eat me if you wished,' he said to the dog as the daggers scraped away at the last of the meat on the bone. 'But I suppose I could eat you too.' He took a bite of his ham.

'I promise not to eat you if you do the same?' Kace said to the dog, extending his hand as if the dog could shake it. Which, of course, it couldn't.

But it could timidly stand and give the boy's hand a small lick. Which it did.

Kace laughed at the sloppy wet patch left on his hand, wiping it straight away.

The dog's eyes were welcoming, so the boy slowly

reached and stroked its soft head.

He realised how small and young the dog looked. *Only a puppy*, Kace thought.

'Me too,' he whispered to the dog.

He stroked the fur once more, and, in one swift motion, as if it had had enough, the dog stepped back, picked up the bone and disappeared into the trees.

'Goodbye to you too,' he called after the dog.

5.

Does the first hair on a boy's chest mean that he is now a man?

Kace sat on the edge of his bed, pulling at the one singular dark hair. It didn't look like much on his pale, smooth body, but it was enough to feel like the first flower of spring.

He smiled and tucked it under his shirt like a medal.

Sunrises and sunsets came and went, and with them, a penny every day. Kace had developed stamina from his milk walks, his calves hardening as the days passed. It was funny; Kace thought that between himself and Sander working, their life would look a lot nicer. But it remained the same, really.

Sander's drinking increased, and Kace found himself rarely asking his father for a penny for his trips to the market. He paid for these himself.

It had been small money in the grand scheme of things, so Kace wasn't too bothered. But when the king's taxman called for his share on the last day of the month, Kace realised how dire the situation was.

'I'll give ye over to the boy,' a resentful Sander said to the man standing in their doorway with his hand out for coin.

Kace stepped forward, feeling small. Feeling way too little to be dealing with this.

'Ten pennies, young sir,' the taxman said in a half-mocking way. Kace could hear the sound of yet another ale bottle being opened behind him.

'I don't have that much,' said the boy truthfully.

The king's man looked up at Sander, who stood cluelessly. Finally, Sander said, 'I expected my son to have it, he's making a penny a day now, you know.'

'I, um, spent it,' Kace said quietly.

'Spent it?' Sander exclaimed. 'What do you mean, *spent it?*'

'I don't have time for this,' the taxman huffed. 'Ten pennies now, or you'll be given notice to pay in a week's time at the cost of twelve pennies.' He looked down at his papers wanting to be onto the next house by now.

'I don't have ten pennies spare,' Kace said quietly.

Sander just shrugged and walked back to the bottle of ale, stumbling into a chair as he went.

'I shall see ye in a week's time then. Good day.' And the taxman was gone.

Kace plodded over to where Sander sat prodding the fire.

'Always keep money aside for the taxman,' he hissed at his son. 'I'm using this as a lesson for you.'

Kace felt his face redden with anger. He turned and made off in the direction of his bedroom.

'What are you even spending all of these pennies on, boy?' Sander called after him.

'Your supper,' the boy spat, slamming his bedroom door shut. Shaking the entire house as he did.

Every Saturday after the first milk run, Kace went into the forest. He would walk the long way around to avoid the playing fields and the suspicious eyes that ran around them.

The dog was there without fail each time.

On the third Saturday in a row, Kace found himself off the fallen tree and sat on the damp, leaf-covered ground, waiting for his friend.

Like clockwork, the bush rustled, and the dog walked out, giving Kace a tail wag.

He named the dog Elex.

The naming process had felt naughty. Like he was breaking some sort of Ellon town law. Which he might quite well be, actually.

'Hi, Elex,' Kace said cheerily.

He imagined that, if the dog could speak, he'd say hi back.

He noticed Elex carrying something in his mouth: a small dead bird.

'Is this for me?' Kace said, half repulsed, half honoured.

Elex dropped the bird at Kace's feet. He suspected the dog was repaying him for all of the food he'd brought.

A dog always paid their debts.

Kace didn't go to the market that Saturday. He spent most of the day in the forest with Elex.

After he had pretended to eat the little dead bird, they played a simple but tiring game. Kace threw a stick, and Elex went to fetch it and brought it back to his feet.

They played this game for hours. Neither boy nor dog got tired of it.

Sander paced furiously, waiting for the boy to get home.

When the door opened, he snapped. Like a coil that had been waiting to spring.

'Where have you been?' He demanded.

'Work,' the boy replied.

'All day? I'm hungry and have been waiting for my supper.'

'I didn't go to the market today, Da,' Kace said.

'You didn't go to the market?' the man said, seething now.

'Yes. That's what I said.'

Smack.

Kace hadn't seen it coming. His father's rough hand came at him and hit his cheek like a rock. If one were standing in the room, it'd be hard for them to pick who looked more shocked. Both man and boy stood a moment. The man with his outstretched hand, the boy with his reddening cheek.

'I'm sorry,' Sander said to neither Kace nor himself directly.

'Da…' Kace tried desperately to hold back the tears.

'I didn't mean it, I'm hungry. I…' he trailed off. Kace hardly heard the rest of it.

Sander pulled his big boots on and just in time, right before the tears came, he slammed the door shut.

Alone now, Kace let the tears come. They were hot and stung his cheeks.

His father must have eaten at the tavern that night because the following morning, when Kace woke, a bowl of stew from The Oak, sat outside his door.
A peace offering, perhaps? He ate the cold stew quickly and went up to the farm.

'What happened to you?' the milkmaid asked, pointing at a darkening bruise on his cheekbone. He touched it, sore to the touch.

'I fell,' he said, looking for the milk bottle labelled Lady Viaol. He found it and, as the milkmaid tutted him, he made off for the house.

The morning walk was his favourite. In the cloak of darkness, he'd find anonymity. The ghosts of the night faded away as the early risers surfaced from their beds. The women who worked the streets at night, the thieves, the night guards all handing over to the bakers, the milk boys, the farmers.

We watched the night, it's your turn now.

Kace liked the hours that belonged to no one in particular. He didn't feel he had to be anything in those hours, yet there he was, working those ungodly hours. How noble. It gave him a sense of pride, of belonging. If only to the one simple task of delivering a bottle of milk across town.

'Good morning,' he said to the groundsman, who, to Kace's surprise, was out of his hut and shovelling a pile of horse mess off of the driveway.

'Mr Kace,' he said, walking towards the boy, 'didn't you hear? Lady Viaol and her husband have travelled north for the races. There is no need for milk today.'

'Oh. Do you want this, so?' Kace offered him the milk.

'It doesn't sit well in my stomach,' said the groundsman as if he was reliving a traumatic memory. Kace found it best not to imagine what said memory might be.

'Take it for yourself,' he said, and Kace made off with the pint of milk.

'Lady Viaol has gone to the races,' Kace explained as he entered with two milk bottles. Sander looked up at it and then back to the tea he was brewing.

'It won't go to waste,' he muttered.

It was hard to look at the boy and pretend his bruise wasn't there. But Sander tried.

Every glance at his second-born caused a fresh pang of guilt and self-loathing.

Finally, when he could no longer stomach the elephant in the room, he submerged a cloth in cold water and pressed it against Kace's bruise.

The boy winced, making Sander's stoic face nearly appear sympathetic.

'So, Lady Viaol is not in town?'

'Nay. Only her groundsman. A nice man,' Kace said, hoping maybe to prod a fit of instinctual paternal jealousy. But the man's face revealed nothing of the sort.

'I won't do this again,' his father said after a moment's silence.

'Thank you,' Kace said.

Kace learnt the first of life's great certainties: the taxman will always return when owed a penny.

He had awaited the visit, twelve pennies in a sack by the door.

Kace proudly handed it over, not expecting a reward as such but wanting to rub it in the taxman's face that he did, in fact, have the coin to pay. Like a helpless win of sorts.

'Thank you, you've contributed to your town today, sir,' the taxman said, placing the sack into his satchel.

'Question,' Kace called after him. The taxman turned to him again.

'Where does that coin go?' he asked, sincerely curious.

'On maintaining the town, of course,' the taxman said.

'But the town isn't very well maintained, is it?'

'I beg your pardon,' the taxman huffed his fat cheeks, 'the king takes excellent care of all his towns.'

'So the money goes to the king?'

'And then back to *your* town. Good day.' The taxman left, his satchel twelve pennies heavier.

Sander had sat at the table watching the entire interaction. 'Good man,' he nodded slowly, 'always keep money aside for the taxman.'

Kace agreed that he would. It seemed that the tax responsibilities were his now.

'And don't waste your breath wondering where it goes.' His father drank the end of his morning ale and left for the workshop.

'It seems stupid not to question it,' Kace called to his father. But he was gone.

That evening, when Kace got to Lady Viaol's house, he was surprised to find the sheriff and two of his men standing by the groundsman's hut.

'Boy!' the sheriff called, startling Kace from his early morning stupor.

'Is everything okay?'

'Not quite,' declared the sheriff. 'State your purpose for being here.'

'I am Lady Viaol's milk boy, sir.'

'I see. The Lady has been robbed in the night. Can you say where you were?'

Kace felt his stomach drop, 'In bed, sir. I was asleep.'

'Can anyone vouch for this?'

'My father would have seen me go to bed. Otherwise, I was alone.'

The groundsman stepped out of the hut, pointing his old bony finger at Kace, 'He is the only person who know that Lady Viaol was at the races.'

'Is this so?' The sheriff said, like this was proof enough. 'I'm going to take you to the town hall for further questioning.'

'It wasn't me!' Kace quivered. 'I promise. I was asleep from just after dark until only an hour ago. Please!'

But Kace was already being escorted away.

Through the town, they walked.

He felt the eyes of everyone they passed.

I always knew there was something off about that boy, they whispered.

Kace heard them speak. Even in the silence.

He's the home-schooled boy, isn't he? Odd boy.

Kace wanted them all to stop looking.

Aye, his brother was the one eaten by dogs, right?

The sheriff pushed Kace roughly into a cell and closed the door with a bang. It took him the best part of half an hour to get his head around what was happening.

Lady Viaol's house had been robbed, and he was being accused of the crime. He thought back to the woman hanging in the market square. It had been a while since a crime like this had been committed in Ellon, but he imagined a similar fate was due for him.

He looked down at his feet and imagined them hanging lifelessly for all to see.

Perhaps he could be spared. Perhaps he'd only be sent to prison. But Lady Viaol was a respectable woman, and her husband was often found in conversations with the king himself.

If word had got to his father—which he imagined it did, enough people saw him paraded through the town by the sheriff— he clearly wasn't in much rush. It was nearly dark when one of the sheriff's men unlocked the door and let Sander in.

The two didn't say a word to each other for a moment. Kace spoke first.

'I didn't do it.'

'I know,' Sander said, pulling his son in for a hug, 'I know you didn't.'

Kace spent three nights in the windowless jail cell. He wasn't too sure if it was day or night when the sheriff finally opened the door and said,

'Kace, you can go.'

'Your weak arms got you off, kid,' mocked one of the sheriff's men as he passed by.

Later he'd find out that the thief could have only entered the house one way: through the thick barn doors that lead to the storage rooms. A twelve-year-old boy the size of Kace couldn't possibly have forced those big barn doors open. So, the sheriff had to let him go.

He liked his job too much to hang a little boy for a crime he didn't commit.

It was as if Sander had known Kace would return soon, for he did not blink twice when the boy knocked on their front door. Hands wrung awkwardly behind his back.

'I'll make you supper,' his father said as he opened another bottle of ale before work. Kace knew he wouldn't, so walked to the market himself, bought some potatoes and fresh fish and went home to cook.

It was clear that the whole town and their   mothers knew about Kace's arrest as the stares were long and hard on his walk to the market.

A curious part of him wondered what they were saying

about him. Another part of him didn't care at all.

In the market square, he looked up at the wooden beams he could well have been hung from.

He bought supplies for supper and then made the walk back through Ellon.

'Lock your doors!' one of the boys mocked as Kace passed by.

'Not funny,' Kace muttered at the laughing boys.

That afternoon was the first time he brought his novel out to the forest. A collision of his two happiest worlds: reading and the forest.

He sat underneath a tree, waiting for his little friend to come.

And he did. Little Elex and his wet nose sniffed his way into the clearing and, upon seeing the boy reading, began to wag his tail enthusiastically.

'Hey, friend,' Kace said, giving the happy dog a stroke. It was hard to believe this was the same dog that froze, terrified, not long ago. The same could be said for Kace.

Elex lay next to him as he read.

The weight of it surprised him.

He moved his book aside to see the dog's head resting on his lap. His head was heavy for just a young dog. Kace had never seen a dog this close, nor had he ever seen a dog close its eyes.

But here, in the depths of the empty forest, this dog closed his eyes and drifted to sleep on the boy's lap.

As he read, he stroked Elex's soft ears. Hours passed. Hours of reading and strokes.

Kace didn't have any food. He didn't feed the dog once that afternoon. Yet, he stayed. Kace wondered if he was staying out of hope that food would appear.

Or did he just like the company too?

He watched as the dog made a little sound. A small bark in his sleep, like he was having the scariest of dreams.

'Shh,' the boy said, stroking the dog harder now, 'it's ok. I'm here.'

The dog woke, yawned, and, as if he was embarrassed, trotted away from the boy.

The dog didn't leave, though. He hid behind the tree and watched Kace finish his book and leave the forest. Like a shadow, he followed him back towards the town. Kace didn't notice his stalker. When Ellon came into view, the dog became more aware; the town was not a safe place for a dog. Kace slipped into the crowds and up towards his home.

'Dog!' shouted a voice, startling Elex. He ran away as the townspeople cried for the sheriff's men and their guns. But the dog was far too quick for them.

The house was empty when he got home. Truthfully, it had felt empty since Brithe had died. The short dog hairs on his trousers prompted him to want to clean. Starting with his clothes, then going onto the floors. He scrubbed them methodically. He washed the soft fabrics of the house and dusted the wooden surfaces. He cleaned until his hands were raw. He cleaned his father's room too. Brithe's things still cluttered the space.

A box. He didn't recognise it, and curiosity took hold of him. He set his dust cloth down and, with a *swoosh,* he pulled it from beneath Sander's bed and clicked it open. It was quite disappointing. Just a collection of lady things. Jewellery, to be specific.

Probably worth a penny or two, thought Kace. But then thought nothing more.

Da's probably holding onto it for sentimentalities sake.

But as he was about to close the box, he recognised something.

A piece that he had seen before, but never on his mother. But he *had* seen it. He was sure of it. It was a rearing horse made of the most striking gold he'd ever seen.

Snap.

Kace shut the box and pushed it back under the bed.

6.

He thought about the box constantly. What's a rich lady with one less box of jewellery when it could keep food on the table for an entire family?

Kace never thought he would be the type of person to turn to religion. But everyone in Ellon seemed to. So, he went to the vicar and asked him a frank question.

'How do you know what's right and what's wrong?'

The vicar set his prayer book down and offered a pew to the boy.

'You ask a complex question with a simple answer, boy.'

He watched the vicar smile warmly. He had never minded this vicar. He was gentler than the rest. He spoke with a simplicity that Kace admired.

'Good is all that God approves of,' the vicar said. 'The word 'good' and 'God' are so similar for a reason, after all.'

'Hm,' Kace started, 'is it really that simple?'

'Why would you not want it to be? Do you not agree that life is too short for making these questions more complex than they have to be?'

'What if life is to find out one's own answer to these questions? Instead of just following the crowd blindly.' Kace gestured around the empty church.

'What a waste of time,' the vicar smiled thinly. 'I prefer a much simpler life.'

'So if someone was to steal,' Kace said, 'that's inherently bad because stealing *is* wrong in the eyes of

God. Even if they stole from the rich?'

The vicar's face grew pale.

Of course, like the rest of the town, he'd heard the reason for Kace's arrest.

'Are you confessing to your crimes?' The vicar's tone had changed now.

Kace puffed up his chest defiantly.

'In the eyes of the sheriff, I am innocent. Do you not believe me, vicar?'

The vicar stared at the boy, softening his voice slightly, 'It would be one thing to steal, but to then go on to lie in front of God.' The clergyman tutted like he'd heard the worst now. 'So, before we carry on this discussion, Kace, think carefully about how you answer this.' The vicar paused.

'Did you steal from Lady Viaol?'

'No.'

'Do you know who did?'

'Yes.'

The vicar nodded a short nod. Then leant forward and knelt.

'Pray with me, boy.'

Kace got to his knees too and, together, they silently prayed. Then the vicar whispered, 'Amen.'

His old, weakened knees caused him some difficulty as he stood.

'Kace, you must live your life as if God is always watching. You must leave and ask yourself what God would want you to do.'

Kace approached the town hall and stopped.

He knew that God would want him to walk in and tell the sheriff it had been his father who had broken into Lady Viaol's house. But if God existed, he had also taken his mother from him. So, he walked home and put supper on.

We're even now, he said to the ether, hoping that God was listening.

As they ate, he asked his father outright. He wanted the truth and only that.

The bulky carpenter sat his fork down and picked up his ale. His fifth bottle of the night.

'Answer me,' Kace demanded. 'Did you break into Lady Viaol's house and steal her jewellery?'

'A man has to make sure he can feed his children. At whatever cost.'

'Hardly,' Kace muttered.

'You don't think I feed you?'

'I meant you're hardly a man.'

Sander stabbed angrily at his meat, making blood squirt onto the wooden table.

'And no,' Kace continued, '*I* put food on this table. And I cook it, too, Da. All you do is drink your money away.'

'You don't know the half of what I pay for, Kace. Don't you sit there thinking you've got the moral high ground because you pay for some potatoes? I pay the landlord. I pay for your education. I pay for the fire to keep you warm. Don't talk about what you don't know, boy!'

Kace was determined not to let tears fall like he

was just a stupid little boy.

The father snarled, 'I pay for the plot of land where your mother is buried. I save money for you, and I buy the bullets that keep our guns loaded. I keep you safe, Kace.'

'You kept me locked away.'

'I keep you alive.'

'This isn't living. Ma is more alive than me.'

'How dare you say that.'

In a notably smooth movement for such a giant of a man, Sander was on his feet and had his son by his shirt collar.

'You have no idea, Kace,' he snapped, with little foamy spitballs flying from his mouth.

Then it happened.

Kace didn't see how the dog had gotten in. He must have followed his nose and known something was amiss inside the boy's house.

As Sander's drunk, meaty hands held Kace's shirt roughly, Elex's teeth grabbed at the carpenter's flailing clothes. The man spun around in a petrified panic.

'Mutt!' he screamed as the dog pulled at his clothes.

'Elex,' Kace said sternly, 'let him go.'

The dog's eyes looked from Sander to Kace and back to Sander.

Then reluctantly, let go of the man's clothes.
Kace knew the dog had to leave. Now.

Sander was panting and stepping towards his shotgun in great strides.

Get out, Kace willed the dog with his mind.

'Do you know this mutt?' Sander said, still backing away slowly.

Get out!

'Da, wait.'

But Kace had only a split second.

This loyal dog was not going to leave without him.

Kace ran towards the dog, tapped his furry head and said, 'Let's go!'

The boy and the dog ran out of the house to the sound of Sander's shouts. Down the wooden stairs and out onto the cobbled streets. Nearly falling as they did.

In the distance, the sheriff was trotting towards them on horseback.

Someone must have heard the commotion and called for him.

Kace turned and ran in the opposite direction with his four-legged friend bounding alongside him.

The baker and his son opened their door, as did a few other neighbours. They knew something was amiss. But they did not expect the sight of a boy and a dog running from the sheriff on his horse and a drunk Sander with a shotgun, following close behind.

The town had talked about *the whore and the mutt* for just a few days. But this sight, of *the boy and the dog*, would stay on their lips for years after.

Some would go on to claim it was folklore. Some would question how accurate those sightings had been. As the story travelled, it became more hyperbolic, passing between tavern doors, details embellished, and moments fabricated.

The dog was the size of a horse, I heard.

Aye, the boy rode the dog out like one might ride a horse. The boy was part-dog, too, I heard.

A town that traded on gossip had just gotten its payday. The proverbial ship had come in.

'The mutt bit me, and the boy stole from Lady Viaol,' Sander cried to the sheriff. 'I found the Lady's jewellery in our house!'"

'He must have used the dog to break through the barn doors,' the sheriff, atop his horse, shouted.

The sheriff kicked his horse to speed up. The loud clops of her hoofs alerted everyone to clear the way. Most of the town was out watching the chase now. The sheriff's horse cantered down the narrow street, rapidly gaining on Kace and Elex.

But the boy and the dog had the advantage of being small. They slipped in and out of the tight cobbled streets with ease.

The large horse couldn't maintain speed on those tight turns, and the boy and his dog slipped further away.

The last person to see them was the milkmaid, leaning out of her cottage; she saw how happy both boy and the dog looked. They were running free from Ellon.

She could only smile and wish them the best.

7.

The forest was a scary place for most. But for Kace and Elex, it felt like returning home.

They wandered with only their footsteps for company.

Once, when Zanty brought a map of Ellon to lessons, Kace remembered the forest to be about the size of a thumbnail.

Already, an hour into walking, he knew that map couldn't possibly have been to scale. It seemed to continue endlessly. It was a sea of trees with branches like waves swaying above him.

He considered turning back, of course, he did. There was dread in his heart about what lay ahead, but he feared more what would be awaiting him in Ellon. He felt trapped in a place neither here nor there. To go back meant certain death. To carry on meant likely death.

He had to just keep walking, and hope. What else can one do?

They had only been in the forest for a few hours when the rain came, bringing with it a sharp clap of thunder and the first light Kace had seen since Ellon.

The rain came down hard, instantly soaking both the boy and the dog through.

He felt the forbidden house looming above him before he saw it. The turrets were like tall statues towering above him. The crack of lightning. The rumble of thunder.

Kace and Elex ran towards the house, up the steps

and banged on the front door. Nobody was in, of course. He felt foolish, as the house had long since been lived in. The creak of the door invited them in. But the house lacked what's needed to be a home. No person was present, a warm fire or even a solid roof.

Save for the occasional lightning streak, it was completely dark. The reverie of the place hadn't lived up to its reality. He'd imagined grand things, alas, this was not. Deception is a vile creature.

He'd walked past the forbidden house countless times, imagining what lay inside of it. A world of new wonders. A place of refuge, but there wasn't even a cover to keep the rain from him.

He turned and ran, away from the house and away from all that disappointed him.

'Come on, Elex!' He shouted, and the dog bounded along after him.

The final crack of lightning hitting what remains of the house. Like a perfect pinprick of penetration, it snapped the place of wonder.

Outside, it still came down heavy. They ran for shelter; a dense tree sat nearly on its side with a heavy, blanket-like covering. They pushed through the greenery and into the dry dome.

'Where are we going to go, Elex?' He rubbed the dog's perky ears. 'Are we going to run, or are we going to hide? I think that I might well know. Don't you?'

But the dog didn't speak back, he only rested his tired head on the boy's lap lovingly.

'I guess you're right,' he said, 'we can make a plan

in the morning.'

He, too, lay his tired head on a mound of moss. The sound of the rain atop the mushroom dome sent them both into a dreamlike state. Both of them felt a concoction of fear and safety. A strange sensation, that. They were simultaneously hyperaware and blissfully calm.

Kace was too on edge to sleep, while the dog was too on edge to relax his ears.

But both were calm enough not to notice the bright green eyes that watched them from the bushes.

He wasn't too sure if it was morning, for the tree they lay under was so dense that the sun could hardly penetrate it. The rain had stopped, and they were dry again, except where the occasional residual drop from the leaves would land. It was his hunger that had woken him, and the thought of no pantry to raid scared him.
Elex was awake and sat like a regal statue, panting hard.

'Morning,' he said to the dog, hoping to ground himself. If he could hear his voice surely it meant that he was still alive. 'What do you have for breakfast out here then?'

The dog cocked his head.

'I am the guest in your home, after all. Where's the bread and butter?'

Elex stood and gave the boy a lick.

'That's your breakfast, is it? A lick of me.'

Elex kept licking, making Kace laugh giddily.

'Stop it!' He rolled over in the bed of moss and laughed as the dog sloppily covered him in sticky saliva.

'Ok, I'm getting up,' he said finally, pushing the dog off him and standing, 'lead the way, Elex.'

The dog did a good job of this. He walked just a few steps ahead of Kace and out to an open patch of grass.

The trees around them were like an impenetrable wall.

'Why are we here?'

The dog made its first noise. A single sharp bark at a row of bushes beneath the trees, and the plump berries that hung there. Like murdered fruit.

Kace looked at them and smiled.

'You're a healthy dog, are you?'

The berries weren't very filling, but they were enough to keep their stomachs from complaining too much on that first morning.

He knew he needed something more substantial. The dog could catch and eat raw meat, but the evening chill was coming, and Kace needed to start a fire.

He started to collect wood, piling it up in the centre of the grass patch. He felt exposed in the open. But at least he could see any predators coming.

That felt more important to a boy born and raised in a town who had no sense of how to survive in the forest.

He piled the wood in a cone shape. He thought this was most appropriate for starting a fire.

He was only speculating, really. But he reckoned if he set the whole pile ablaze, he'd have a warm, roaring fire to cook and live beside.

The next thing was to source water.

From the memory of Zanty's map, a large river ran through the forest with various off-shooting veins.

It started at a waterfall and went all the way down to Ellon. Kace had no idea how to find this water, but he hoped Elex might lead him there. Dogs need water too.

After several failed attempts, he managed to start a fire. It had only been crackling a small ember when he was flung to the ground with a thud and tasted grass. Elex barked wildly at whoever had just tackled him to the floor. He shouted, but nobody would hear.

Someone was stamping out the small flame, and when Kace came to, he looked up at a pair of very green eyes.

'What are you doing?' Kace exclaimed.

'What are *you* doing?' The stranger replied. 'Fire causes smoke, and if they see smoke, they'll come!'

'Who will come? Who are you?'

The stranger gave Elex a quick pat on the head to settle him, unafraid of the dog, Kace noted.

'*People* will come,' she uttered.

'People?' Kace asked, looking at the stranger properly now. She must have been just a little older than him. Chestnut hair in messy waves and a few lonely face freckles.

The royal blue hair bow she wore stood out aggressively against her bright green eyes.

'People,' she said like it was the most obvious thing.

'And who are you?'

'I might ask the same of you,' she said defiantly.

'I am Kace, and this is Elex,' he said, pointing at the dog who sat by the girl's feet calmly, assured this was not a dangerous situation.

'Nice to meet you both,' she said sincerely, 'I am Adiana.'

She started to retreat to the trees as though she'd said too much.

'That's a nice name,' Kace called after her. But she was gone. Just like someone had blown her out.

Who was she?

Why was she in the middle of the forest too?

He began to think that perhaps he had made it up entirely. He doubted his sanity and realised that he needed a drink of water. Maybe he was delusional. Water cures most.

Finding a vein of the river had proved easier than he thought. Maybe things were starting to look up.

He simply walked briefly in a random direction, hoping a plan would come to him, but, better yet, the sound of running water welcomed him instead.

He sat on a rock and shovelled large handfuls of water into his mouth. Glancing for the green-eyed girl, constantly.

Beside him, Elex, too, lapped up the water. Water flew in all directions from his busy tongue.

'This whole river, and you must splash me right here,' Kace said, wiping the river water from him.

Drunk on water, they wandered upstream to an eroded water pond on the river's bend. In it were slimy silverfish swimming stupidly in circles.

'Dinner,' Kace said, smiling at Elex, who must have had a similar thought as he bounded into the pond and pathetically tried to catch the quick-moving fish with his uncoordinated mouth.

'Elex, here, boy,' Kace said, worried the fish might escape back out onto the river's current and wash down to where the Ellon fishermen were waiting.

Obediently, Elex ungracefully climbed out of the water and shook himself dry—and got Kace wet in the process.

Catch the fish, cook the fish, supper.

But Kace didn't know how he would go about catching a fish. Elex's efforts, although unplanned, were at least an attempt. Kace just stood there staring at them, as if a rod might magically appear if he stared hard enough.

The dog soon grew tired of the boy's reluctance and jumped back in.

'Yeah, that's what I would have done too.'

Somehow, Elex managed to catch one of the silver slippery fish.

'Yes, boy!' Kace shouted. 'Good boy.' He petted the happy dog and looked at the floppy fish. The dog looked up at Kace as if to say, 'Give him some dignity, at least.'

'I can't!' Kace said, realising what the dog was asking of him.

The dog nudged the fish further from the water it was trying to flop back into. Kace sighed and picked up a rock. He looked sadly at it and, with one swift motion, ended the fish's struggle.

He wandered on, carrying the dead fish by the tail. Repulsed at the trail of blood that dripped behind them.

In a clearing of the trees, at the far side, stood a tall wooden tower. Man-made and with a small balcony at the top.

He went over to it and marvelled up at the weedy tower. Inside, a spiral staircase led all the way up to the balcony. He stepped on the stairs and they started to give away. The wood splitting in the middle.

Maybe not. He left the tower and found Elex sat waiting with the fish.

'You knew not to go in, didn't you?' Kace asked the dog, 'What else can you teach me?'

Kace ate berries for supper that night.
Elex had a lovely fish.

The following morning came, and the hunger was beginning to become painful.
He picked a few berries as Elex chewed happily on a stick.

'You're going to have to eat something you kill,' the girl's voice said.

Kace turned to see the bright green eyes looking at him again.
'Where did you come from?'

'I've been watching you. To make sure you don't start another fire.'

'What people will come?'

Adriana stood and walked towards Kace.
'The people with sharp axes and loud voices.'

'Do you live in the forest?' he asked. She only laughed.

'I live near the forest. Only stupid people would live *in* the forest.'

Kace felt that this was directed at him, so he shrugged.

'I like the forest.'

'So do I,' she said, 'I come here to hunt, drink and bathe. But I live somewhere much safer.'

'And where's that?'

The girl seemed hesitant at first. 'Why do you want to see my home?'

'Sometimes friends visit each other's homes, you know.'

Adiana seemed to think about this for a long moment like she was stuck on a moral conundrum.

'Fine,' she said finally, 'Get your dog.'

She turned to leave, quicker on her feet than Kace.

'Why do you trust me?' Kace called after her.

They continued on through the forest; Boy, Girl and Dog.

'Because you tried to start a fire in an open patch of trees. You're hardly a threat,' she mocked. 'Plus, my conscience. If I don't help, you'll be dead before sunset tonight at this rate.'

Adiana was nimble on her bare feet, like she knew every step she had to take. She led the boy and the dog out of the forest in a dance-like way, up the hill to a cliff face.

'Do you live up there?' Kace asked, looking up to the top of the cliff.

'No,' she said, pointing to a cave at the bottom of it, 'in there.'

'You live in a *cave?*' Kace said in disbelief.

'It's the safest place to live.' she huffed, and he followed her, putting his life in her hands.

Kace couldn't help but smile. His new friend was

allowing him into her safe place. Not only that. But the *safest* place in the forest.

He caught her looking at his smile, and like a beautiful infection, it spread to her. She smiled a very thin smile.

Adiana cleared her throat. 'Shall we?'

The cave had very little; a makeshift bed, a black pit of burnt wood and a shabby chic table made from a dried-out tree stump.

The bed was the most prominent feature of moss and foliage sat in the corner, it appeared to be all the cave was used for. Sleeping. Kace pictured Adriana as a little bird collecting the twigs to make it. Looking at her, he realised how much she reminded him of a bird, actually. Those bright green eyes zipped from thing to thing. Her short arms, like little wings.

'How long have you lived here?'

'Hm...' The girl thought as she picked moss off a log. 'All I've ever known is this forest.'

She chucked a dry log onto the cave's centrepiece: a pile of burnt ash and wood.

'I thought a fire out here is dangerous?' Kace said, half mocking, half genuinely wondering.

'Out there, it's dangerous, yes. In here, they are not,' she said. 'The smoke seeps through the cracks and releases on top of this cliff slowly. The fire itself is hidden by the cave.'

She prodded the growing flames with a long thin, burnt stick. 'A fire out there is asking for trouble. A fire in here is survival.'

Elex liked the cave, too; he sat by the fire and closed his eyes, tired. The warmth began to dry his coat properly for the first time in a long while.

'He looks happy here,' Adiana said, sitting on her mossy bed.

'It's sheltered. That's probably more than he's had before.'

'Is it more than you've had?' She asked, perhaps sarcastically. He couldn't tell.

'I had a nice home with a soft bed,' he said, his gaze lost in the fire. His eyes went into a dreary sleepy state. The sting in his eyes made him want to lie on the moss bed and sleep until he had a plan.

'So did I,' she said.

'I thought you lived in the forest your whole life?'

'No. I said that all I've ever known is the forest. There's a difference.'

She didn't tell him much more than that. Instead, she declared,

'You can stay—but only for a bit. Just until you figure out what you're going to do next.'

'I might be here a while then.'

'Don't you have a plan?'

'Do I look like I have a plan?'

'No, but you could be being deceptive.'

'I guess I'll just wander with no destination in mind,' he mused.

'Oh, don't do that,' she said, 'that's how one dies in the forest.'

The dog made its second noise; not a bark this

time, but a loud, nasally snore.

The sound echoed off the cave walls and bounced back to the sleeping dog, startling him awake. Both Kace and Adiana laughed loud as the dog's ears drooped back, seemingly embarrassed.

'Silly dog,' Kace said, rubbing Elex's ears.

'Tomorrow, I'll teach you how to catch a fish.' Adiana said, settling deeper into her moss bed.

Next to her, Kace was staring at the cold stone floor.

'You look puzzled?' Adiana asked.

'I am trying to find the most comfortable place.'

Adiana pulled at the old and torn blanket atop her moss bed, 'you can lie next to me here?'

Kace's face reddened at the thought. Like she knew what he was thinking, she rolled her eyes.

'Friends can share beds. It's not *just* for marriage.'

Kace shuffled forwards and lay down next to this odd forest girl, relaxing into the mossy softness as he did. He was glad of the place to relax.

In the black silence, Kace spoke, 'I don't want to kill a real animal.'

'Who determines what a real animal is?' she asked rhetorically.

'I don't know?' He felt clucless. 'I just don't want to kill an animal.'

'Surely you've eaten animals before? In this lovely home you supposedly once had.'

'Of course, I did.'

'So what's the big difference in killing it yourself?'

'There's a difference. I'm not a wild animal.'

Kace could hear Adiana smile as she spoke; 'Yeah? Are you so sure, Kace?'

8.

The next morning, Kace killed a fish.

'They're stupid,' Adiana said, as she talked him through spearing the fish.

'Is that the justification? The lower the intelligence, the less guilty you feel?'

'It helps,' Adiana said.

Kace picked up the freshly dead fish and looked into its lifeless eyes. 'No emotions behind these eyes,' he said as if he was trying to condone himself.

'We'll cook it tonight.' And with such ease, she speared another silverfish.

'You make it look easy,' he remarked.

'I've done it a thousand times.'

Based on that, he tried to calculate how long she'd lived out in the forest, foraging her own food.

'Adiana, are you happy?'

'What's that supposed to mean?'

'I'm trying to understand you.'

'You say that as if anyone can understand anyone.'

'Don't you want to understand me?'

'Not really.' She was casual but not mean in how she spoke. 'I've seen enough people come and go.'

'Out here?' he said, surprised.

'Where's Elex?'

He realised that the loyal dog no longer sat with them on the river's bank.

'Elex?!' he called.

'Don't shout!' She hissed, digging her nails into his

forearms.

'How else will I find him?' He said, trying not to show the pain her uncut nails caused him.

'Let's look,' she said, standing and picking up the two dead fish.

Kace tried to remain calm, while she seemed perfectly at ease.

'The forest will always give it back to you,' she reassured him, 'whatever *it* is.'

'Elex…' He shout-whispered so as to keep the girl happy. Whatever she was afraid of was no joke to her.

'He's probably off hunting a rabbit,' she said, this time softly stroking his forearm with her fingertips.

'It's not like him to wander off, though.'

They searched for an hour, not straying too far from the spot he'd wandered off from.

'He's a dog,' Adiana said. 'Dogs wander.'

'I know. At least, I think, I know. I don't know dogs.'

'He's got a nose that can find us,' she said.

'Not if he's been shot.'

'We'd have heard a gun. The forest is a very quiet place.'

As the sun got lower, Adiana became more on edge. Her tranquil nature giving way to tension. 'We need to make our way back to the cave,' she said, looking at the distant dark approaching.

'Not until I find Elex,' said Kace defiantly.

'Kace, this is not a place to wander at night.'

They began to walk back in the direction of the

safe cave.

'He's a wild dog, Kace. He will be okay.' She said, saddened at the thought of his friend feeling sad.

Adiana slowed by a tree with a mushroom-shaped dome draping down to protect an enclosed space. Adiana parted the green vine leaves and stepped in.

Inside, thick intertwining root-like branches wrapped around a thick central stump, little wood chippings paved the floor. It was a serene space.

'This is a Danyan tree,' she said, touching one of its protruding branches, 'also known as the wish-fulfilling tree.'

Kace stepped forward to the tree and marvelled up at the size of the green dome above him.

'There's a belief,' she continued, 'that if you enter a Danyan tree's enclosure, and whisper your desires to its trunk, the forest will grant it.'

'In exchange for what?'

'Nothing directly,' she said, 'but the forest will only fulfil your wishes if you are a noble person, you see.'

Kace moves his mouth close to the thick trunk and hoped that he was a noble person.

'Hallo, Danyan tree,' he whispered, 'I'd like my dog back by my side, please.' He stepped back, hoping the tree worked efficiently.

But nothing happened.

'What now?' He asked.

'We see if you are a noble person,' Adiana said, stepping out of the dome.

Kace was silent for the duration of the walk back to

the cave. But his eyes darted around for the dog.

While hers were looking for predators.

'What are you so scared of?' Kace asked as the fish crackled above the cave's continuous fire, 'out there in the forest?'

'Death,' Adiana said gravely.

'What's out there?'

She prodded the fire absentmindedly, 'Kace, if you're out here long enough, you will meet them.'

'What if I miss them?'

'You won't.'

Kace hoped that he could stay awake in case Elex returned in the night, but the very nature of the cave made it hard to access. Especially at night. So, he let sleep win and promised to return to the river the following morning.

He dreamed of Elex running through an empty field, being chased by an angry horse. Kace desperately tried to run in his dream. To run to Elex. Alas, he couldn't.

At the first sign of light, Kace was eager to get back down to the river.

'Where are your family?' he asked as they walked like he was trying to distract himself.

'I must have had a father, but I never knew him. Mother left a while back and never returned.'

The nonchalant way in which she said this took Kace aback. Was she not concerned?

'Your mother never returned?'

'Aye, I'm not too worried, though. She'll come back. Or she's dead, and I'll see her in the next life.'

'Do you really think there's another life?'

The girl looked at him with a sudden fire in her green eyes. 'Of course, there's another life. Why would you question it?'

Kace shrugged.

'I hope you're right,' he said sadly.

'Why would you not want there to be?'

'I mean, there's no proof that there is,' Kace said.

'That wasn't my question,' she said, 'if our brains can comprehend a utopic eternal afterlife where we reunite with all we've lost, why wouldn't we? How blissful that is.'

'Won't it be a disappointment if you die and it's just nothing?'

Adiana shrugged, 'Well then, there will be nothing, won't there? So I'll hardly feel it, will I?'

'But if a utopia afterlife exists, surely there must be an opposite. An eternal suffering?'

'Why must that be so?'

'Because that's what the church teaches,' Kace said obviously.

'Are you to just follow that blindly, so? Sounds awful restrictive to me.'

'So, you say that a person can pick and choose what they want from religion?'

'Why not?'

'That heaven can exist, but hell can't?'

'Why not? Do you have any proof of anything else? My interpretation is as good as a vicar's. Both I and the King himself could speculate on an afterlife, both of us will have the same amount of evidence.'

'But the king represents God's watch over us?'

'Do you really think that?'

'No.'

She paused a moment, 'Then don't.'

They sat for a long moment in silence, Kace churning over all that he once knew. It seemed so simple, the thought of choosing one's own beliefs. But it felt like a relief in ways.

'Who did you lose?' Adiana asked softly as they reached the edge of the river.

'My Ma too,' he said, looking around for any sign of Elex.

She didn't ask much more, and they walked on in silence.

They heard his bark first. A sound so pleasant and familiar that Kace's heart nearly melted into his stomach upon hearing it.

'Elex!' he cried out, as the dog bounded towards him. Adiana smiled as the two reunited. Her eyebrows were raised too, clearly surprised at seeing the wild dog again.

'Where did you go, silly boy?' Kace rubbed him heatedly but in the loveliest of ways.

'I guess you are a noble person,' Adiana said smiling.

She hunkered down next to the boy and the dog, 'He's got blood around his mouth He must have gone off to hunt.' She pulled his lip up, revealing his teeth stained with fresh blood. 'The fish and berry diet clearly wasn't enough for him.'

'What do you think he ate?'

'Rabbit, probably. Or a fat bird,' she mused, looking at the proud dog.

'Could he kill us?' Kace asked unprompted.

'Of course he could.'

'But you wouldn't, would you?' Kace said resting his forehead against the dog's.

They walked along the river's edge. Kace happily throwing a stick for Elex to chase.

'The forest always gives back,' he mused.

'It does.'

And they walked on to nowhere in particular.

*

In a gambling house in Ellon, people were busy placing the most vile of bets.

'Two pennies that the boy's body gets washed up in the harbour,' a man slurred drunkenly to the man behind the bar, who suddenly looked nervous.

Sander sat in the shadows, a pint of ale in his meaty hands.

'If he doesn't get eaten by his own dog first,' the drunk man continued.

The barman shot him dagger eyes to stop talking. But it was too late. Sander grabbed the drunk man by the back of the hand and smashed his head onto the bar's counter.

Sander slept in his second home that night: the town hall's jail cell.

The people of Ellon mocked him for having a

dog-loving son.

The irony, they joked, *his first boy was eaten by a dog. His second son ran away with one.*

Sander had spoken very little to anyone since Kace had run from Ellon. But he'd been in enough fights to last him a lifetime.

Nobody came to his workshop anymore.
The townspeople didn't trust him and his cursed family.
He'd had to close up the shop just days after he tried to return to normal. He even tried to sell it, but nobody would buy it.

It might be cursed, said one of the local property men. *Nobody will touch it with a stick.*

Sander's meaty hands now fought drunks in Ellon's worst gambling houses instead of making furniture like they used to.

*

Kace missed his father the way one misses a childhood imaginary friend. He missed the version of Sander he'd created in his own head. The one he fabricated from the good.

Sander had once been a good man. Or, at least, not a bad man. That was quite enough for Kace, really. He'd never expected the world—he just wanted a small piece of Sander's.

Enough to show that he cared the way a father should. But increasingly, Sander had only pulled away further. Until the night they ran. Now he couldn't help but wonder whether his father had searched for him. This must be his worst nightmare. A son wandering the forest alone.

'I feel guilty,' Kace said, needing to release a thing into the world.

'How so?' Adiana asked.

They lay in a field with the sleeping dog next to them.

'I feel like I've done something stupid.'

She gave him the space to gather his thoughts, perfectly content in silence. At first, it had scared Kace, but now he began to enjoy it. He liked the slowness of it.'Do you know when someone loves you, and you know they do, but it's the wrong type of love?' he continued, feeling foolish for saying so. He couldn't imagine this green-eyed girl knowing anyone.

'Love, but the wrong type,' Adiana said back, trying the words on for size.

'What am I saying... What do you know about love?' Kace scoffed, realising that he sounded crueller than he had intended to. She looked hurt, making Kace realise that this strange forest girl had more going on beneath the surface. Of course, she did. Doesn't everyone?
He felt like a fool for thinking otherwise.

'Is a crisp white dove still beautiful with a broken wing?' She asked. Her green eyes looking longingly out to the forest.

Kace's eyebrows must have given away his confusion as she scoffed slightly and told him when he knew the answer to that, then maybe he could forgive his father.

He didn't have to wait that much longer to meet what Adiana was so fearful of in the depths of the forest. It had been that evening, walking back to the cave when they met it.

He hadn't seen it at first, but both the dog and Adiana did. They were much better suited to the wild, with eyes sharper and way more adept at spotting them.

'Kace,' Adiana said coldly, in a tone that he'd never heard her use before.

'Kace. Don't move.'

He didn't, but he scanned the surroundings for whatever beast was ahead, fearful of the sudden change in both the girl and the dog.

Elex crouched to the floor like his four legs were melting away. He lay as flat and still as a table.

'Do not move,' she whispered. 'Not an inch, Kace. Not a single inch.'

He heard it before he saw it. The hissing sound of a stalker's tongue.

When he finally saw what was coming towards them, he felt his stomach drop. The way it moved along the floor, the length of it and its eyes gave him goosebumps.

'It can't see us,' Adiana whispered. 'It hunts on vibrations. So, stay still.'

'Can't we just kick it?' he whispered, half with a fearful laugh, half sincerely wanting to.

'No,' she snapped back quietly, 'it'll be back with its fangs in you before your foot gets back to the ground.'

'I assume it's, um…'

'Very,' Adiana whispered, knowing what he was

going to ask. 'One bite from that, and you'll be dead in moments. Hardly a moment to say your prayers.'

The snake went very still and silent, suddenly.

'It's going to pounce,' Adiana whispered.

'At us?'

'We're about to find out.'

'Do we run?'

'No.'

'Why?'

'Because then it will go for us.'

The wait was agonising. Then it all happened quick.

The snake shot forward like it was coming from the barrel of a gun, and it slunk it's fangs into the body of a bird sat picking at a berry tree.

The snake ate the bird whole, and Kace felt ill at the sight of the still alive bird's bulge slowly moving down snakes tube body. Until it stopped moving.

The snake scanned its surroundings for more. Before slowly moving away and up the trunk of a tree and into the deep foliage.

Adiana let out her breath slowly, 'I suspect one of them got my mother,' she said.

Elex shook himself like he'd just come out of water. Trying to shake off the memory, Kace supposed. Both the girl and the dog carried on walking like all was normal again.

But Kace felt a deep fear for the mundane way in which the girl had acted around the poisonous snake. He felt the forest's dark side reach out with bony fingers. Offering its hand. It was like a blue sky that turned grey.

Adiana, walking on, felt his fear radiate off of her back. 'I remember seeing my first forest snake,' she called.

She turned to his rigid body.

'You get used to them.'

She smiled like all was normal in the world again. Which for her, it was.

But Kace couldn't help but feel that he didn't wish to get used to them.

9.

Sander spent yet another night in a jail cell. This time for attacking a boy that had written *dog lover* across his now closed workshop doors.

The boys had sat sniggering in the bushes. Sander had managed to grab one of them by the collar and gave him a few too many smacks. Not enough to do too much damage, but just enough for the sheriff to get involved.

He'd attacked many of the Ellon men but, this time, the law couldn't look past the age of his victim. Not that Sander would ever describe the ratty little boy as a *victim*.

'You can't go beating up kids,' the sheriff said, like it was the most obvious thing.'I know.' And he did. Sander knew how stupid an act it was.

'You shouldn't drop to their level,' he urged, signing Sander out of jail for the second time in just a few days.

'Aye,' is all Sander could bring himself to say.

As he walked from the town hall, the sheriff called back after him. He pulled Sander away from the town hall and towards a stall selling hot brews.

'I fancy a cup,' the sheriff said, offering Sander the opportunity to join him.

They sipped from their ceramic cups. Sander felt glad of the burning warmth inside of him. It was like all the bad inside him was being burnt away.

'I know a man. He's not cheap, but he's discreet and thorough. He's in the business of hunting. Legal hunting, don't fear.' The sheriff looked around to ensure that they were alone.

'Hunting dogs, so perfectly legal. But he specialises in finding *particular* dogs. He's part tracker, part hunter. He knows the forest like a childhood home.'

'Could he find my boy?'

'He could find the mutt that ran with your boy. Find the mutt, find the boy.'

Sander took the man's address on a scrap piece of paper and pocketed it.

'And if I get him back to Ellon...?' Sander asked, fearing the answer as he did.

The sheriff shook his head slowly. 'Lady Viaol is too powerful. I can't get him off for his crimes.'

Sander drained the end of the hot liquid. *Burn guilt. Burn!*

'I could make a plea to the king. Ask him to pardon the death penalty. He'd be sent off to jail though. He'd spend his life there.'

'A life in the forest or a life in jail,' Sander wondered aloud.

'I don't envy you having to make this decision.'

Sander fingered the paper as he walked.

Most of the town tried to hide the glances they stole. They were too polite to stare.

Some didn't opt for subtly though.

On the way home, a drunk shouted at Sander: 'How's your forest boy?' He had a fat smirk on as he did too. A smirk that made him look punchable.

A few moments later, the sheriff was interrupted while packing up for the day.

'Sir?' One of his men said.

The sheriff knew what was coming next, he'd only just let the man free.

'Sander has just beaten a drunk on the street.'

The sheriff sighed. 'Bring him back in then.'

*

Out in the forest, Kace was standing completely naked in fast-moving water. The water's white foam bubbled and moulded around his ankles.

'Don't turn around!' he called out over the sound of the rushing river.

'I won't, but there's no need to be so precious,' Adiana called back. By the inflexion in her voice, he could tell she was smiling as she said this.

He had made the mistake of asking how one washes in the forest.

'You get naked and wash in the river, of course,' Adiana said like he had asked the most stupid of questions.

'I'm not getting naked with a *girl* around,' Kace said, unable to control the blushing.

But Kace, suddenly aware of his odour, had agreed to it so long as they kept their backs turned from each other at all times. Adiana rolled her eyes and called him a wimp.

'How do you wash at home?' she asked, naked too,

in the river.

'I wash in the tub, of course,' he called back, dabbing his arms with the cold water and trying to hide the wince as he did. A lot was to be said for the warmth of a bath.

'In your clothes?' Adiana asked.

'No, we have a door,' he mumbled. 'For privacy. It's civilised.'

'No one can see you out here,' she said. 'Isn't that just the same as a door?'

'But you could turn to look at me!'

'Someone could open a door?'

Kace huffed and watched Elex bounding through the water.

'See, he doesn't mind showing himself off,' Adiana mocked.

'He's an animal,' he remarked.

'You seem quite sure of the difference, don't you?'

After they'd washed, they dried themselves in the sun. Kace self-consciously adjusting the clothes that lay across his lap for dignity.

Despite their *nakedness,* Kace felt comfortable with his new friend. To sleep alongside her and to bathe, albeit moderately privately, with her felt intimate. But not romantic intimacy, sibling intimacy, or even parental intimacy. It was its own unique special little thing. He'd finally told her why he was running.

The truth of who he was and why he'd run with Elex had hardly made her bat an eyelid. He suspected she had lived a life not too dissimilar. An outcast. Made to run out of fear but also the want for liberty. The strongest of cocktails. And he was drunk.

He knew their bond couldn't last though.

He needed to keep moving. As nice as this had been, he was beginning to realise that he wasn't destined to stay in the forest forever.

'Adiana,' he turned to her naked beside him, unsure of where to look, 'tomorrow, I'm going to head to The King's town.'

'Why?'

'I need to be closer to a new beginning.'

Elex perked his ears like he was listening too.

'You can't bring him into a town...'

Kace looked at the loyal dog, 'I know, but if I can get somewhere where nobody knows me, I can keep him nearby and safe while also having a place to live.'

'And you think the King's town is that place? Surely, if word gets to Ellon that you're there, the King will hang you personally in his own garden.'

'The King's town is big. It's busy, and I can have the anonymity of the forest but in a busy place.'

'You'd abandon him?' Adiana stroked the dog's ears, like she was trying to cover them..

'I want bread,' he said, 'and I want a warm bath with soap, and, um, privacy.'

She looked hurt. 'Don't you want to stay here with me? Don't you want to be my friend forever? Our friend?' Adiana grabbed weakly at her clothes and covered herself. He was surprised by the sudden closing up. It was like she'd suddenly become human and aware of her nakedness.

Elex looked at Kace like he, too, was asking the same as her.

'It's complicated,' Kace said quietly.

It wasn't, really. The forest had tested him. He'd never even been a fan of fish, but now it was all he ate. Along with berries that were often too sour. Fish and berries. That was all he ate.

Rabbits had been easy to catch for Elex but far more of a challenge for Kace.

The encounter with the forest snake had reminded him of his own mortality. It had scared him so madly and deeply that he wanted to run for hills, and that was the problem: Kace always wanted to run.

And here, he had plenty of reasons to.

A man who has known luxury for his life will think of anything below it as primal.

But the sad truth is that he hadn't even known luxury. He'd only known a basic life but compared to this life in the forest, it had been the grandest of times.

To sit at a table with a roof over one's head and eat a stew that had been cooking for five hours, with a slice of the baker's fresh bread, was the epitome of luxury.

Adiana didn't say much that evening. She huffed plenty and rolled over to sleep on her mossy bed without saying goodnight.

He hadn't planned to sneak away but in the early hours of the morning, Kace silently gathered what little possessions he had, gently woke Elex and crept out of the cave. A far less dramatic exit than the night he left Ellon. But a departure that pained him more.

Adiana would wake in a few hours, and what would she think? Would she stand at the mouth of the cave and look out into the vast sea of trees to try and find him? But he would be long gone by then, claimed by the forest.

*

On a dark street, Sander glanced over his shoulder to make sure nobody was following him. Why would they be? Paranoia makes all shadows appear darker than they are.

He took a sharp turn down an alley. Behind wooden shutters, eyes glanced at him. *Who are you?* They wanted to know. He'd never been down this particular alley. Most in Ellon avoided it like it was not even there. Only the most questionable of characters lived down there.

He found the address. It was a basement flat. He could see the door; down a flight of stairs, below ground level. Sander knocked with his most confident knock, feigning that he was still within his comfort zone. He may look tough, but he felt far from it.

A man known for selling potent hallucinogens scuttered past on the street above Sander's head. He carried inconspicuous vials of dark-coloured liquids.

But the man that opened the door to Sander was not at all what he expected. Sander was flustered all of a sudden, assuming he had gotten the wrong address.

'Sorry, I'm looking for Duxos,' he told the man. He must have been only five feet short.

'Aye, who sent you?' asked the small man.

Sander cleared his dusty throat and dropped the name the sheriff told him to use.

The small man nodded curtly and stepped aside, 'I'm Duxos.'

'I'm Sander,' he said, stepping into the grungy little flat.

The small man smiled, his teeth yellow and cracked. 'I know who ye are, Sander. I suppose you want me to find yer little boy?'

The space inside Duxos flat was too small for Sander's wide body. But for Duxos, the room was all perfectly proportioned.

He was skinny too, with no muscle. It made him look like a child. Sander couldn't quite understand how this man could hunt and kill a vicious hound.

On the wall were two dog heads, stuffed and mounted proudly above a roaring fire.

'My first kill,' Duxos said, after following Sander's eye line to the dog, 'and, beside it, my biggest kill. Two of my proudest.'

Sander nodded his approval. He stared at the evil eyes of the two dogs on the wall. Vile, cruel things.

'You know who I am?' Sander asked, as he sat on a chair that was a bit too small for him. He felt the fabric cupping his fat arse. The support felt nice, actually.

'All of Ellon knows you,' Duxos said. 'Even before your boy ran off with the *mutt.* 'How he said this last word made Sander realise that he had come to the right place.

'Can you kill the dog and bring my son home?'

'I can find them, and I can kill the dog, yes. I'm not

in the business of kidnapping children, though. Not very lucrative.'

'I can make it lucrative.'

Duxos looked up at Sander, studying him closely. 'How much is it worth to you?'

'One hundred pennies for the dead dog and the boy back in Ellon.'

'A hundred pennies is a lot,' Duxos pondered, then leant forward to speak slowly. 'If you were to source me a vial of something to drop into the boy's water and he was to become, let's say, *temporarily incapacitated,* I could then do my civil duty and return him to his father.'

Sander nodded along silently.

'And I'll kill the dog in the process,' Duxos said, smiling like that was only for his pleasure.

Sander thought of the man he'd seen walking in the alley. The man with the little vials for pain, for pleasure, for excitement. For incapacitation.

'Deal,' Sander said, extending his hand. Duxos met it with his little bone fingers.

*

His feet were sore just an hour into his early walk towards the King's town. Kace and Elex slowly plodded their way through the thick forest. Each step brought with it the fear of a snake. He wanted the ability to hover above the ground. To glide without disturbing the ground where they were lying in wait with their sharp fangs.

If Elex was worried about snakes, he hid his concern and happily bound from paw to paw as they walked. He'd occasionally wander off, or follow a bug inquisitively, then trot back up alongside Kace again.

'I thought you'd gone back there,' he'd say to the dog, who would say nothing back.

'I don't blame you,' he said to Elex, and perhaps to himself, 'if you want to go back. Why would you walk into the unknown? Why would anyone?'

He'd ask this, but continue to walk anyway. Constantly worried if he was doing the right thing.

'What are we doing, boy?'

He found himself asking that a lot lately.

*

Duxos tied a bag strap tightly around his shoulders. A small handgun in his holster bounced against his thigh while a bigger shotgun rubbed against his back. He walked towards the forest. He carried only supplies for a few days and enough ammunition to kill every dog he saw enroute to finding the boy. And that was something he *was* going to do. At all costs. He was going to find the boy.

10.

Right foot. Left foot. Right foot. Left.

The walk north was monotonous. Kace became bored of the hike by hour three of day two. One of the only things that saved his mind was the constant change in danger. At first, he thought the snakes were his biggest concern, but the further he walked into the dark forest, the more danger that showed itself.

It was the smallest things that scared him the most. The little insects with sharp stingers, the buzz of the poison-filled bugs. He recognised a lot of them from his lessons with Zanty, the books she brought with diagrams were coming to life here in the forest. The shapes that were once sketched on paper now crawled and flew past him in real-time.

The temperature scared him too and, as he climbed, the cold would attack at night. He hadn't even gotten a blanket, so he lay shivering with only the heat of Elex's furry body to keep him warm. *Snakes are cold-blooded,* Adiana had said to him. *They don't mind the altitude. Fewer predators.* Kace thought about this repeatedly. The nights on the climb were the scariest. Snakes and cold temperatures waited to kill him.

He had a rough idea of the route. Get as high as he could, over the mountain range that bowled around Ellon's forest and then drop back down to the valley on the other side. Continue through until he reached the biggest river. Find a way to cross it and somehow scale the town wall.

Without a horse, the trip north was suicidal and slow. Few had done it by foot. Kace didn't fancy his chances much, but something about having Elex by his side gave him a sense of purpose and a drive to survive. If he could keep Elex safe, then, he too might survive the journey with only a few light stings or a couple of branch scratches.

Elex, with his triangular ears and fuzzy tail, represented hope. And hope is all a person needs at times.

On a particularly cold night, the sound of a rustling bush startled Kace up. He was frozen in the pitch darkness, unable to see past his nose. This is why Adiana hadn't wanted to be out at night. It all made sense.

Elex froze momentarily, too, and sniffed the air inquisitively.

The bushes continued to shake, whatever it was was coming closer. Kace held his breath and remained as still as he could.

The shaking stopped then and Elex bounded forward wildly. The squeal of an animal filled the dark night, and Kace, panting, hunched down, and wished to be in his reading nook in Ellon.

In the morning, a dead badger lay bloody on the forest floor. Elex, with blood around his mouth, looked as proud as could be.

Kace felt the vomit rise from his stomach, and he leant into the bushes to be sick. To know he'd slept the night in the dark next to the mauled animal made him feel sour.

*

Duxos hoped that the hunt would be quick and painless.

The task was a simple one: walk into the forest he knew so well, track the dog, drug the boy and bring them both back to Ellon. One dead and one alive.

He'd hunted more difficult hounds for pleasure. This was a job, easy by nature but difficult to keep quiet. When he brought the boy back to Ellon there would be a frenzy about him. Duxos wasn't wanting the town's attention, in his line of business it was preferable to act like a shadow. Delivering the boy in the cloaked darkness of night seemed to be the only way not to cause a stir. But those thoughts were for later. Now, he must find them.

As he went deeper into the forest, he hummed a tune. *Every* time he went into the forest he hummed aloud the same tune. It started innocently, many years ago, just as a simple melody stuck in his head. But the first time he was attacked by a snake in the forest, he noticed that he hadn't hummed his tune that morning. It quickly became a superstition. He *needed* to hum the tune as he climbed through the bushes around Ellon's playing fields and entered the forest. It was an offering of sorts, he thought.

He had only been walking an hour when he came across the first signs of the boy and the dog. A berry bush picked near raw, far too empty to have been a bird or a dog alone. This had been the work of a hungry boy. Duxos smiled as he hunched by the bush; paw prints and human footprints were dented into the mud. This would be far too easy, he smirked to himself hungrily.

In a clearing ahead, a small badger came into view. It shuffled along the forest floor, carefree.

For no reason but just to do it, Duxos aimed his

shotgun and squeezed a bullet out into the badger's head.

*

Adiana couldn't stop thinking about Kace and his dog. It had been two days since they snuck out of her cave and down into the forest. Everything felt damp without them. As much as she didn't wish to admit it, he had been nice to have around. A friend to talk to was such a simple luxury.

As she slunk around the forest, going about her usual routine of hunting and building, she heard a familiar sound. The man that hums the same tune. She froze on the spot, and through the trees, she saw him plodding along, carrying a gun that was far too big for him.

She watched as he stopped and crouched by a berry bush. He prodded the mud with his skinny fingers and smiled. What thoughts was he having, she wondered.

She had watched as he aimed his gun at an innocent badger and shot it dead.

The little man stepped over the dead animal and left it for the maggots to feast on.

Adiana found herself wandering north, not to follow Kace as such. She couldn't leave the area she knew so well. It was too dangerous to venture from her part of the forest.

But a mischievous part of her wanted to test how far she was willing to go. She flirted with the boundary of her safety. Just teasing it slightly, then retreated to the cave she called home.

*

Right paw. Left paw.

The climb was endless, and even Elex was beginning to suffer. He looked up at his human, wondering where they were going. He trusted this person. He had never had any reason not to, but why were they walking so far? He had to trust, though. That's all a dog can do.

Kace had hard red blisters on the bottom of his feet. But the pain almost completely disappeared with the monotonous walking. The constant repetitive action of step after step dulled it like a natural painkiller.

Onwards, the boy and the dog walked. They stopped every time they encountered a vein of the river, swallowing the water until they couldn't stomach it anymore. Who knows when the next body of water would show itself?

Kace would bathe his sore, hot feet in the cold water, relieving them even more, while Elex would bound into the deeper water and paddle about to cool himself. The walking was hot, while the nights were cold. The boy wasn't comfortable, ever. The dog, a wild animal, more naturally took to the elements.

When they got close to the peak of the hill, they began to see the distance they'd climbed. He could just about make out Ellon in the distance, down the steep hill and across the sea of trees.

He marvelled at it. The town that used to be his entire world was oh so small. The scale of the forest surrounding it engulfed its seriousness. The thousands of trees, like little king's guards, about to attack the town.

He fantasised about it. How easily the trees could pillage Ellon and all that lived in it. The thought both terrified him and pleasured him.

While panting next to him, Elex licked his lips with his large, wet tongue. Kace wondered how old the dog was. He mustn't have been too old at all. He looked like a young adult. Not quite pup enough to be mothered, but too young to have the wealth of experience of an older dog.

He petted the dog's soft head, then traced his fingers to his mouth. He pushed up the draping flap-like lips around the dog's mouth to reveal his sharp teeth.

'You really could eat me all up,' Kace mused. But Elex's reassuring gaze, with his large chocolate eyes, put the boy's fears to rest.

'Let's get some sleep,' Kace said to both the dog and himself. They made camp in a now empty burrow. It looked like a pack of something had once caved a circular, enclosed home here, but the dog's willingness, after sniffing it thoroughly, to lie down suggested that whatever had made this hole was long gone.

So, they curled into each other, as familiar as brushing one's teeth before bed. The dog's slow breathing brought the safety of a bed. He felt endlessly grateful for the dog. His saviour, his protector.

When Kace woke the dog was gone.

At first, Kace assumed he was at the breakfast buffet: a small rabbit hole he'd sniffed out the previous night.

But as the morning sun grew brighter and became

warmer, he began to worry that the dog wouldn't return. They had to start making a move if they were to find a place to sleep that night. To stay in one place in the forest was to sign his own death warrant.

'Elex!' he called out of the hole they'd called home for the night. 'Elex, boy?!'

He knew Adiana would scold him for shouting into the forest, but he wanted his dog.

Back outside, he followed the pawprints to a bloody circular patch in the twigs. Elex had probably just caught a rabbit. Nothing much more than that. His heart sank at the thought of anything else.

'Elex?' he shout-whispered to the nothingness.

Only the sound of a faraway waking bird. A buzz of a bee. No dog to be seen or heard.

Kace packed up what little possessions he had and began the day's walk. The dog could and would have to find him. He couldn't stay here waiting for death to come. He had to rely on the dog's nose to reunite them. He had to trust if the dog could do it once, he'd do it again.

He made his way up a particularly steep hill and over slabs of slippery rocks. Concentration was needed to keep him from losing his footing and ending up in between two boulders. He worried about Elex following his trail, would the dog be able to navigate his way over the rocks safely?

Kace feared the dog might find the rocks too challenging, so he needed to incentivise him. Something to show the dog he was on the right track. He grimaced at what he must do.

He found a suitable rock, dropped his torn, raggedy trousers and began to pee against the rock. The smell only his dog would know as his. A few metres further, once clear of the rocky terrain, Kace picked some berries and scattered them behind him as he walked on. *I'm going this way, boy,* the berries were there to say. Little juicy red signposts to help the dog along.

He wondered how long his clothes would last him and, when he got to the King's town, how he would afford to buy new ones. He didn't want to think of anything less than the comfortable bed of an inn. But how would he make that a reality? It was an expensive place, the King's town, and dirty scrawny boys like him would stick out like, well, a dirty scrawny boy in a royal town.

These were all later problems, he told himself. He'd figure it all out, surely. First, he just had to get there.

He felt a sting above his ankle, so gently touched it, the red-raw sting already protruding a small white bump.

He looked all around, there were low-lying thick vines of watercrumb leaves. He figured he must have been stung.

He anxiously pictured the balloon-shaped teacher and began to look in the trees for sugarcane.

Sugarcane won't come up in your exams, you don't need to know about them, Zanty had said once.

Wrong, I absolutely do need to know about them, Kace mused as he searched.

He found a tree that he didn't recognise and snapped a chunk of its bark off of the trunk. Inside, a clear, gloopy liquid trickled down and out.

Kace rubbed his sting with the gloop and instantly felt its relief.

Education will prepare you for the future, they all had vsaid.

*

Just a few miles back, Adiana was stalking the little man with the big gun. He had headed north, prodding at various footprints in the mud. Inspecting broken branches and snapped twigs.

How the man moved intrigued Adiana; he was like a baby rabbit in his movements. The way in which he hopped from foot to foot and left no trace. Harmless on appearance, but harmful on knowing.

She'd heard him whistling through the forest many times, with the occasional gunshot following his arrival. They often were the only two humans to roam the forest around Ellon, but only one knew of the other. He didn't know of her existence, and she wished to keep it so.

She followed him. How good a tracker can he be if he didn't notice the light-footed girl behind him?

*

Sandwiched between Adiana and Kace, Duxos was sure he was on the right path. He reckoned he was about a day or two behind the boy. The footprints were only that fresh. Not much more.

Truth be told, he expected to find the boy sooner.

He thought the scared little thing would be hiding in the thick of the forest, barely surviving. Glad of the rescue.

But, clearly, he was healthy enough to travel. Up a hill, no less.

Duxos settled down for the night by the rocky terrain. Right on the spot where Kace had peed the day previous. It was like the ghost of the boy was mocking his stalker.

Duxos took a big sniff in through his nose holes. *Clean forest air,* he thought.

He took an apple from his rucksack, peeled it and readied himself for sleep. He didn't like to consume high amounts of food when he was out on the hunt. The weight of meat sitting in his stomach slowed his thinking. It made him feel *ploddy.*

So, he'd starve himself whilst hunting, the primal need to catch and kill drove him to work at his peak.

The painful gnawing in his stomach burnt from the inside. But it was worth it. This was the only way he could hunt.

Tiredness took him and led him to sleep.

*

On the other side of the rocky terrain, Kace, hungry too, settled for the night. Odd, he thought. Where was Elex? He couldn't be too far behind, surely?

Kace had only been asleep an hour or so when the shotgun startled him awake. Like an explosion inside of his brain, the sound was deafeningly angry. He sat up, heart racing. A shotgun. Where did that come from? Here, in the forest? He wasn't alone, he realised all of a sudden. The unmistakable sound of the gun in the darkness was as telling as a human voice. Somebody was on the other side of the rocks.

Kace gathered what he had and quickly made a run through the darkness further up the hill. Whoever was out there would have to cross the slippery rocks in the darkness to get him. He knew he had time to put some distance between himself and the person.

As he ran, the fear came in three waves. Who was out there shooting in the darkness? What were they shooting? And where was Elex?

11.

She had watched it all happen in a three-beat rhythm.

One, two, and three.

The bush shook, the little man grabbed his gun and squeezed out the fatal shot.

One, two, and three.

Despite knowing it was coming (if only for a split second), the sound made her jump high into the air. Her skin prickled in fear too. Her brain told her to run, but she had to stay and watch.

In the milky silence after the gun had fired, all she could hear was her own heartbeat—so loud that it was like it was in her neck. A gunshot in the silence was never easy to get used to. It signified man was about. And there was nothing more dangerous than man. Even here in the forest.

The little man, as calm as anything, walked up to the now-dead shape and kicked it over onto its back. It rolled slowly at first, then gravity took hold and showed its belly.

As cool as if he'd just gotten a seasonal letter from a relative, he discarded the empty bullet shells and began to make his way across to the rocky terrain. If he was planning to stay the night on this side, he'd clearly had a change of heart. The little man was on the move.

Adiana didn't usually go beyond said rocks; that was the boundary of her comfort zone. Metaphorically and physically.

But, without so much as a glance back to her cave, she made her way to the rocks and walked onto them like they were on fire. One gentle step at a time. One, two, and three.She stepped over the dead snake. The poison leaked from its fangs and pooled next to its cold blood.

*

Kace felt he was high enough and far enough away from the source of the gunshot. He settled himself again and decided it best to rest his feet. He knew sleep was impossible in his heightened state, but he could at least relieve his tired legs until the sun came and lit the path ahead.

And when dawn finally did arrive, it brought with it the most spectacular of sights.

A simple sight, but one so beautifully executed by Mother Nature. It was like she'd signed the bottom right-hand corner of the beauty herself. The fangs of light pierced through the trees and, in the early morning haze, Kace could hardly help but feel a sweet sorrow. It was the most beautiful sunrise Kace had ever seen. The air tasted as if it had just been picked yesterday.

It was that calming beauty which reminded him of why he had loved the forest so dearly in the first place. The feeling that nothing else matters except the oxygen there before him at that very moment. To swallow a breath meant he was alive and, oh, what a beautiful taste that was.

He took a few deep, slow breaths in and, for the first time since falling into the forest, he found himself smiling at the little things. The harmless insects fluttering by, busy starting their morning too. The soupy drip of dew off of the trees down onto the floor below.

And Elex.

There he was, tongue out, ears flapping as he ran towards the boy.

'Elex!' Kace cried, dropping to his knees to greet the dog and his happy tail. 'Keep up with me, boy! You're too slow!'

Whenever the dog returned, Kace felt the same warmth of comfort he had when he first met him.

And so, both the boy and the dog began their walk for the day.

'Where did you go?' Kace asked the smiling dog as they meandered through a particularly potent-smelling field of flowers. Elex sneezed a dramatic sneeze with his wet nose, making the boy laugh. 'You can't tell me where you went, can you?' Kace said, suddenly becoming aware of the dog and its own life. 'Where is your family?' he mused aloud. 'Are you alone, or did you go to visit another dog? Am I taking you from them?' Kace stopped suddenly.

'Oh, Elex, boy! If you have a family, you mustn't leave them. Is there a ma or da Elex?' he exclaimed to nobody in particular.

If the dog understood, he didn't care too much. All he did was sniff a flower, unaware of the boy's concern, and sneezed again.

'I hope that I'm not leading you from everything to nothing. I hope there is something at the end of this.'

If the dog cared about where the boy was taking him, he didn't show it. He plodded alongside Kace willingly as they went up and over the steepest part of the ridge and instantly back down again.

At the top, Kace stopped to be sick as the height of the ascent took its toll on him. He retched loudly into the bush as Elex lay panting next to him. Like a drunk man's wife, the dog obediently waited for the vomiting to cease.

Kace felt the pain in his head come on instantly. As a matter of urgency, he needed to drop altitude and find a drink of water. He spat out large, solidified balls of phlegmy saliva.

'Don't look, Elex, I'm disgusting.'

And they carried on, dropping metres as fast as they could. Truthfully, Kace found the descent more of a challenge than the way up. Concentration was required to keep a stable footing as gravity pulled the boy and the dog down.

Elex slipped a few times. Having four paws on the dusty terrain gave four separate opportunities for slips to occur. And he slipped about four times. One per paw.

Kace looked like a bird with extended wings as he tried to balance himself. Tipping precariously from side to side. Flirting with falling, but never ending up on his bottom.

By dusk, he'd levelled out and found a small spring of running water. It wasn't a river, but just a little off-shoot of the river's vein. Hardly noticeable to anyone except Kace and his trusty hearing. He'd come quite adept at locating fresh water. There were obvious signs, such as damp ground, buzzing wildlife, and emerald green grass. But it was his ears that stole the show. Like a dog, he was in picking up the tinkle of running water. And when he heard it, he followed it like he *was* a hound on the hunt.

First, Kace let Elex drink. He watched the dog's long tongue scoop up buckets of water.

'Leave some for me, boy,' he said, getting on all fours and letting the small stream of water lap against and around his open mouth. He felt weirdly primal.

After the drink, they (mainly Kace) decided it was a decent spot to camp for the night. Both dog and boy kept waking up desperate for water, so to be near a stream was a necessity.

Kace gathered a few large leaves to sleep on. He drifted into a state of reverie about how nice it would be to have a bed to lie upon. *Soon*, he thought. *Soon*.

*

Wild animals are most vulnerable at the spots where they drink.

Predators instinctively know that their prey needs to come and drink. Why chase and exert valuable energy when one can just lie in wait?

The eyes that watched Kace settle into sleep belonged to a little man.

Another pair of eyes watched the little man watch Kace. These were bright green and alert.

Oh, Kace, they said, *you're making this too easy for him.*

*

Duxos had seen the boy and the dog high up on the ridge's peak. The sound of Kace vomiting had made him smile. *Nobody can hack the forest as I can.*

He had pursued them for the remainder of the afternoon, like a swarm of insects represented by one singular mass. One small, bony singular mass.

When he watched Kace gathering the materials for sleep, he chuckled to himself slyly.

Got you.

He hunched behind a thick bush. Perfect cover. The plan to drug the boy seemed harder now that he stood in front of him. He could shoot the dog with ease. That was the first part of the plan. But get the boy back to Ellon? That would be more of a challenge.

The boy lying like a stupid slab of meat made it all the easier, though. He hunched and considered all of his options.

He hadn't seen the thick tree stump coming at him. He only felt its deep hard *thunk* against his head.

*

Adiana knew she had to act quickly. So, she had picked up the moss-covered stump, snuck up to Kace's stalker and *thunked* him as hard as possible.

The following sounds came quickly; the little man's yelps of pain, the dog's loud barks, and the sound of Kace startling to his feet.

'Run!' Adiana shouted at Kace, who was becoming all too familiar with the dangers of the forest, and didn't question the request.

Kace's eyes widened as he saw the little man with the big gun lying dazed on the forest floor. He thought it looked like he was drinking it all in.

Kace, Elex and Adiana ran into the thick forest. And Adiana slipped away from him, 'I'll distract him!' She called.

He could only protect himself now.

Unsurprisingly, the dog stayed with Kace.

While Adiana, meanwhile, as fast as she'd entered the scene, departed it.

*

They ran through the thick trees and straight out into a clearing, where they ran into a rock-hard obstacle.

Elex had stopped in time, his breaking ability more impressive than the boy's.

But the obstacle had knocked Kace back in his tracks. He fell painfully onto his bottom and stared up at the looming obstacle.

A wall.

It was like no other wall he'd seen in his life. It was taller than any building in Ellon. It was made of fat bricks, tightly wedged together by hardened cement, and seamlessly smooth.

A fortress, he mused up at the sight, this can only be the King's Town.

He'd made it to the King's Town. He had reached

his destination alive.

Just about.

His brain, in some sort of self-defence way, cleansed the memory of what had just happened, and he sat in the present moment, no longer fearful of what was behind him.

He took it all in, stunned. Then he cried, whether they were tears of joy or uncontrollable disappointment, he wasn't too sure.

But he just let them come.

12.

The entrance to the King's Town was how he had expected it to be: tall and heavily guarded. Alert men with long guns.

Kace first had to find a place to leave Elex. Who, in some weird way, seemed to know that his human was leaving him.

'I'll come out to you constantly,' Kace reassured the dog. 'It'll be like when I was back in Ellon.'

Elex rested his chin on Kace's lap as he stroked the dog's soft ears.

'I'm not leaving forever.' Kace seemed embarrassed by this. He stood and petted the dog one last time. 'You're braver than me.'

He slinked towards the waiting line of horses and carts outside of the town's gate. Behind him, Elex's big chocolate eyes watched him walk away. Then he turned and slinked back into the cover of the forest.

Kace cursed the world in which he lived. He wanted *his* dog to be free to roam by his side. What a beautiful luxury that would be. And what an amazing world that would be to live in.

Kace climbed under the thick tarpaulin of one of the cargo carts as quietly as possible to not alert the horse. He tucked himself into a ball and breathed as shallowly as he could. Minutes felt like hours. But eventually the horse pulled its load, and its stowaway, forward.

'Stop!' shouted one of the King's men from outside of the cart. Kace held his breath for so long that his fingers went an odd purple.

The sound of the guard's gloved fingers untying the tarpaulin came.

'Just a search,' he told the cart driver, who grunted something back.

But the guard's fingers stopped, and the tarpaulin remained closed.

'Dog!' The guard cried out.

Outside the cart, the men's feet scuttered away as they went to try to find the dog. Kace let out the smallest breath. Good boy, Elex, distract them for me. Just be safe.

And the horse pulled forward again into the King's town, tearing him away from the forest and the dog.

At a factory outbuilding, the cart stopped, and Kace jumped from beneath the tarpaulin.

Kace felt wildly aware of his look. His torn clothes, his mucky face, his messy hair.

Around him, everyone was dressed well. Like they were all off to a ball.

He couldn't stay like this for too long.

Someone was bound to alert one of the King's guards to the dishevelled boy walking the regal streets. And they'd ask him questions he didn't care to answer.

He would be brought to a jail cell.

He'd be sent back to Ellon.

He must bathe and change his clothes.

Golden lampposts were chiselled with horse heads and floral patterns. It all looked very grand.

He walked to a small inn just off the factory road.

The attached tavern had the lowest beams Kace had ever seen inside of a room. Despite his size, he felt the ceiling constricting him. He couldn't imagine how Sander would have fared in that room.

The woman behind the tavern bar handed out a disgruntled look towards Kace as he entered. There was only one soul in the tavern, a grey-haired man sat in the corner with a whisky bottle sat on his table. He, too, looked up at Kace when he entered but quickly returned to his bottle like nothing was amiss.

The barmaid lay her dirty cloth aside and leant forwards, 'We don't give out free food. Before you ask.'

'That's not what I was going to ask,' Kace said bravely. He surprised himself with how sure of himself he was being.

'Is that so?' The barmaid said suspiciously.

'I've come looking for a job, but instead of full coin, in return, I only ask for a bedroom in your inn and a penny or two for my troubles.'

The barmaid looked him up and down, 'You're not quite dressed to impress, are you?'

'I've been roaming the forest for quite a while,' Kace said honestly, 'I just need a place to rest my weary head.'

She laughed, revealing a row of gum behind a façade of just a few teeth. 'And what skills do you have, forest roamer?'

'I can cook, I can clean, I can run errands, small or big. I'm quick on my feet. I used to work as a milk boy, you see.'

The nearly toothless woman looked up at the whisky man in the corner, it appeared he'd been listening to the whole conversation.

'What do you reckon, Jaisax?'

The whisky-drinker, Jaisax, leant forward to the candlelight on his lonely table. Kace noticed his eyes at first, but soon got carried away to his cheek. The ugliest scar he'd ever seen divided a wrinkled eyelid and a patchy sideburn. It was like his cheekbone had forced its way out of his face through the skin.

'Give the wee boy a chance,' he said and leant back into the darkness.

The barmaid extended her hand. 'I'm Flavia.' Kace shook it as confidently as he could. 'I own and run the bar. I'll be your worst nightmare if you so much as look at the coin box, let alone stick your grubby hands in it. You are not to talk to any punters. You'll start by cleaning. Two hours every day. I'll give you a room and a penny a day.'

Kace nodded along, he didn't care what the terms were, he wasn't going to stay for long. This was only until he could move on to something else. A means to an end.

The boy smiled and looked proudly across back at Jaisax's table. But he was gone.

*

By the boundary of King's Town, Duxos stood watching the carts come and go.

Freshly chopped tree trunks came from the forest.

Soon to be made into everything from tables and chairs to

children's toys.

He feared that the boy had gone in beyond the walls. To catch a boy in a busy town was *not* set up to be an easy task.

The bruise on his head was turning a disgusting blacky blue. He rubbed at it tenderly. What a smack it had been. He had rattled over who had attacked him. He thought the boy was alone in the forest.

He looked over his shoulder, constantly on edge that another moss-covered stick was coming his way.

The King's guards seemed to be out in force that afternoon, so he buried his two guns deep beneath a thick bush. He walked towards the gate, taking out his fake papers and preparing to show them.

'Hold!' one of them shouted at him. Duxos smiled warmly and handed over his travel documents. They were believable. He was just a lonesome traveller from Ellon who had come to watch the King's team play Crossball. That was all.

'Best team in the land,' Duxos said, buttering the guards up.

As he entered the town, he saw two guards flanking a lone prisoner. A homeless girl, by the looks of it. They made eye contact, and Duxos couldn't help but feel sorry for her.

*

After Adiana had helped Kace escape, she retreated to the cover of the forest. The little man was still out somewhere in the forest. Kace had seemingly run straight in the direction of the town's wall.

She knew it would be oxymoronically the safest and most dangerous place for him. And because of the former, she had let him go.

She had watched the little man come back around from the attack and, as he started in the direction Kace had run, she loudly snapped a branch to distract him.

He'd doubled back on himself, sweeping the area she knew Kace not to be. She had climbed a tree and watched him from above. He hissed to himself and then turned back towards the town walls. She could only hope that her distraction had given him enough time to hide the dog and get to the other side of the town's wall.

The lack of a gunshot or a boy's cry for help suggested that it might just have been enough.

Slowly and with featherweight footsteps, she left the forest and approached the town's gate. She watched the guards make their way to inspect one of the carts.

She didn't see the hole.

The ground simply gave away beneath her. She cried a short, stifled howl at the pain that had radiated through her ankle.

'Dog!' One of the guards called out at the sound she'd just made.

She heard the footsteps of heavy boots run away from the gate and towards her. She had to think quickly.

Her nimble feet were her best asset. But the pain prevented her from being able to dodge the men.

They grabbed her roughly. They exclaimed at the sight of her. For she was not a dog.

'What are you doing out here?' They shook her violently.

She could hardly see past them, but she could swear she saw a boy-shaped tarpaulin entering the town on the back of a cart.

At least, she hoped she did. It could easily have just been a sack of potatoes.

Inside the town's wall, she awaited transport to the jail cell. What would happen to her, she didn't wish to think about. She lay drooped like a leaky bag of flour on the floor. She hoped Kace wouldn't be seen.

Two dishevelled children wandering the King's streets would hardly be seen as a coincidence.

They debated on what to do with her, asked her questions about where she'd come from, and where her parents were. She didn't answer, so they sighed and told her she wouldn't like where she was heading if she didn't cooperate. She remained silent, unsure of what to say.

The King's town was not wanting a dirty, homeless child wandering about, and with no other option, they did what kingdoms do, and hid it all beneath a figurative rug.

Adiana looked up at the town's gates swinging open and, like he was the King himself, Duxos walked in.

He must know that Kace is in here.

She watched him, his little snake-like eyes caught

hers. She saw his features make the worst face they could possibly make: pity.

A sudden realisation washed over her; the two of them, the hunter and the prey, were now confined together by walls.

And those walls were planning on squeezing them all some more.

13.

The inn bedroom was below a normal standard.

A dusty desk.

A mouldy bookshelf.

An oil-streaked mirror.

But most importantly to Kace, a bed. Albeit a musty one. But a bed, no less.

It had glistened like a lake in the sun, the soft fabrics, the springing mattress. Kace begged his legs to take him to it quicker. Lying back, the dichotomy of firm softness offered an invite to sleep.

Wash first, thought the boy, forcing himself up and over to the silver tub in the corner of the room.

He ran the water as hot as it could go, stripped naked and lowered himself like a dying lobster. The heat of the water burnt away the cold from deep within. It felt like chunks of thick ice in his veins were melting away. The blood began to flow freely once again.

Few things in his short life had been as pleasurable as that first bath after his time in the forest.

When he finally pulled his red, raw body from the water, he dizzily wandered towards the bed and fell asleep as soon as he touched the fabric.

It was the best sleep he'd ever had.

The following morning, Kace woke with a jump. The darkness of the room tricked him into thinking he was still deep in the forest. He flustered about his surroundings.

A bedsheet. A pillow.

He deflated a slow reassuring breath, feeling a whole lot lighter as he did. He was torn. Part of him felt calmed by not waking in the forest, while the other thought the exact opposite. The lack of birdsong didn't tell him that he was safe but instead, quite the contrary; that a predator had killed everything in the night. The silence of a bedroom scared him for the first time ever. Nature's way of telling him all was all right was blocked by the thick bricks and the tightly thatched roof.

He needed cold air and the sound of a bird, so he stood and walked to the window. Despite it still being dark, he found the crack of the distant sunrise a relief. The first few chirps from the morning choir told him that all was going to be fine.

He walked into the tavern's kitchen early that morning.

'We deep clean these pots every morning,' Flavia told him. 'That's your first job. Scrape off the thickened mess and wash them so clean you'd let your ma eat from them.'

Kace looked away for fear that his face may give away too much. But of course, like any good barmaid, Flavia was astute to a person's mood. She always knew when her regulars were sad and needed a soft word and a hard drink.

'Or whoever,' she said, nicer this time. 'The point, Kace, is that they're as clean as you can make them.'

Kace nodded obediently.

'This is important,' she continued. 'If you don't clean this to a standard I expect, then you're not coming back tomorrow. There's an empty bucket there to fill. Go out to the back alley to keep the dirty water off of my kitchen floor.'

And Kace did. He took the bucket, filled it with warm water and soap, and sat in the rat-infested back alley.

First, he scraped off the hardened food and used a piece of cloth to scrub it. The work was methodically mind-numbing. In truth, it was exactly the type of work he didn't want. The repetitive scrubbing took him easily into a state of reverie where thoughts of Elex and his father lay waiting.

The faster he scrubbed, the more he was hoping it would erase the thoughts. His nails cut, and he began to bleed. *Go away, Da. Go away!*

Flavia appeared behind him. 'Kace, stop.'

Kace, panting now, turned to her, the blood trickling down from his fingernail and into the cook's pot.

'That's counterintuitive, Kace. You can't clean and bleed on the pot.'

'I'm sorry,' he whispered, using the now dirty cloth to clean up his own trickle of crimson blood.

Flavia sighed and took the pot from him. 'I'll finish this. You empty the bottle bins, okay?'

Kace went to the large wooden box of now empty glass bottles. With all his strength, he took it out of the kitchen and down the alley to the large communal bins.

With a crash, he smashed the glass bottles into the bin. He continued one glass at a time.

Smash. Smash. Smash.

He smashed them harder and harder.

Louder smashes filled the alley.

SMASH.

Until, finally, the glass bottles had been fully emptied from the wooden crate into the large bin.

Silence. A lovely, creamy silence.

Kace looked back to the tavern's back door to see Flavia sitting busily scrubbing the pots.

'Feel better?' she asked with a smile.

Kace let out a sharp breath and told her that he did.

Cleaning pots and pans were not his thing but, as his first day of work went on, he found plenty that he was good at. His tight body lent itself nicely to being able to squeeze into narrow spots. Places that the plump Flavia couldn't get to herself.

He squashed behind beds and cupboards in the inn's rooms, pantry shelves in the tavern's kitchen, and just about anywhere a small boy could fit.

Flavia smiled at his little legs dangling from beneath the four-poster bed in the inn's largest room. 'Ye are but a wee cleaning mouse.'

'I'm glad you could find a use for me,' he called out from under the bed, coughing on his dusty feed.

'My allergies are no good for doing a job like that,' Flavia said.

Kace knew it was more likely that her round body and stumpy arms were more likely to be the cause for all the dust in these tricky spots.

Just before evening fell, Flavia paid Kace his first coin and, with it, the boy went off to the cheapest clothes shop he could find. He still managed to get himself a new shirt and a pair of thick cotton trousers for a penny.

With access to hot water, a bed to sleep and now a new change of clothes, Kace was starting to feel human again. Only then could he begin the next step in his plan.

In a serendipitous way, his plan began to fall together like a satisfying jigsaw.

One morning, Flavia asked him outright if he had any documents should the King's Men come to inspect her tavern for any, to quote her, 'runaway boys'.

Kace simply smiled from one corner of his mouth, telling the landlady all she needed to know.

'It's not in my interest to have ye working here without documents,' she mused.

Kace watched as his new employer thought up a plan within her round head.

'Jaisax, can get you papers,' Flavia said, 'should you wish to have a new name and your birthplace be here?'

Kace nodded a slow yes, unsure if this was a trap.

'Leave it with me,' Flavia said, returning to her cauldron-sized soup pot.

Whatever may come from that, he didn't know. But papers would be a godsend, for then he could easily slip out of the town to visit Elex. And crucially, re-enter not stowed away beneath a dirty tarpaulin.

'What's the deal with Jaisax?' Kace asked. He'd seen the old man with the scar inside of the tavern most mornings, until it got busy in the evening and he'd disappear out into the night. He would drink nearly a full bottle of whisky every day. He didn't need to speak to Flavia when he entered the tavern. She'd obediently reach into the wooden crate kept behind the bar and produce his bottle for the day.

'He drinks away the pain,' Flavia mused.

'What sort of pain?' Kace asked.

Flavia looked like someone who had uttered too much of another man's secret. She wiped her dirty apron down and smiled thinly. 'Never you mind.'

The mystery of Jaisax only grew in young Kace's mind. Like any little boy, his imagination ran away with all sorts of grand scenarios that the old man could have found himself cut so horribly on his face.

Fighting for the King.

A duel with a snake.

A wrestling match with a mystical beast.

Kace wanted to know it all. He offered to help Jaisax, constantly calling by his table to see if he needed anything. Anything to get to know the secretive man. But his lips remained as tight as if they had been sewn together.

*

Hidden in a nearby inn, Duxos sat in candlelight, plotting his attack. 'Get the boy,' he hissed aloud to the empty bedroom.

A knock at the door startled him. He stood and tucked the tea-stained papers away underneath the desk.

On the other side of the door stood the innkeeper's son, 'Letter for you, sir,' the kid said, handing over a small envelope.

I hear you've made yourself comfortable in the King's

Town. Is this where my son is?

Duxos wondered how Sander knew he was here. The last thing he wanted was for Sander to arrive and scare the boy away. He had him trapped within these city walls. This was the chance to find him and follow him straight to wherever the dog was too.

Duxos picked up a pen and began to write his reply.

He is still in the forest. I am only in this town briefly, as my gun needs more ammunition.

Duxos hoped this would be enough for the moment. It would have to be. He tucked the note inside an envelope and found the innkeeper's son.

'Get this to Ellon.'

*

In a jail cell in Ellon, Sander sat awaiting his response from Duxos. He paced, hoping it would be today or the following day when word got back to him.

The Sheriff had been oh-so accommodating with the whereabouts of the dog hunter. Sander's slow-growing friendship with the most important man in Ellon was proving useful. And he was prepared to keep beating those who spoke foul of him and his son to continue to spend nights with the sheriff. A man of the law on his side was a valuable asset.

*

In a jail cell in the King's town. Adiana paced the dark dungeon. It was empty, cold and not for the faint-hearted. Luckily, this was no different to a rough night in the forest. If anyone could stomach it, it would be her. It would have to be.

The King's men mocked her like she was only a weak little girl who would die within a few days.
But Adiana was not about to let them get the satisfaction.

*

Just outside the King's Town's wall, Elex lay panting after a particularly exhilarating chase with a rabbit. His stomach was full, and he needed a drink.

But he knew it best not to leave this spot.
His human was sure to return soon.

14.

On his first day off from working in the tavern, Kace wandered the back streets of the King's town aimlessly, looking for something to do. He had three pennies in his pocket and a desire to spend them.

He found a small barber shop and sat in the leather swivel seat excitedly. His first haircut in quite a while.

'Scissors all over, chap,' he said to the old barber, who grunted at this *child* calling him chap.

The sensation of the cold scissors licking his scalp made him tingle. He longed for a hug from his mother. Like an urge, he wanted to run out of the barbers and find her. But she was nowhere out there.

He stared at himself in the barber mirror. Lost in a staring contest with himself. His skin looked older than twelve years old. Stress will do that to a boy.

The thought hit him like a flash of lightning: he was beginning to look like Sander.

The resemblance was minor at the moment, but it was there. For the briefest of moments, he thought about his father being twelve years old. The thought made him all sorts of sad.

'Four pennies,' the old barber said, tearing Kace from his reverie with force.

'Uh?' Kace gulped, 'I only have three pennies, sir.'

'Sorry, *chap,*' the old barber smirked.

'Can I drop the fourth penny in tomorrow?'

'No, you can't. I'll be closed 'morrow.'

Kace didn't wish to do what he did next.

Alas, he did. The time in the forest had made him nimble on his feet. To keep up with Adiana meant he had to be able to hop away from danger.

Before the old barber could grip the boy's shirt collar, he was out the door and down the narrow street.

'Oi,' the barber called after him, 'stop that boy!'

But Kace had slipped away. The weight of guilt unbalancing the three remaining pennies in his pocket.

He wished not to be a criminal. He didn't care for the lifestyle or even the lack of one. On his way back to the tavern, he passed the fortress within the town, the prison. He stared up at the tall brick tower and the steep steps to the dungeon. He didn't want to end up there, from deep within, there were the screams of a woman. Harrowing, scary screams. He promised himself that would be the last crime he'd commit. From now on, he would be as clean as the pots Flavia scrubbed.

*

Adiana was beginning to hear things. See things. Feel things.

They hadn't fed or watered her since her arrival. She was beginning to go delirious. The presence of Kace nearby overcame her, and she began to scream for him. But he did not come.

Instead, the mocking guards came, and finally, after getting their fix on watching her struggle, they brought her some water and bread.

Both were finished before the guards had finished locking the cell again.

*

It was a particularly quiet day at the tavern, and Kace found himself mind-numbingly counting bottles of ginger ale on the bar's shelves. Flavia had stepped out to the market to get some supplies. She had recently just begun to trust him to look after the bar alone. If only she knew of his recent crimes.

A storm was due to roll in, so few people were expected to visit the tavern.

One, two, and three bottles.

Jaisax sat still in his usual seat, at his usual table, drinking his usual drink. Kace glanced at him continuously, keen to talk to the man.

Don't talk to Jaisax, Flavia had told him on many occasions.

He didn't know why he wasn't allowed. But he needed his job and a place to sleep. He couldn't risk losing it all by giving in to his curiosity. But sometimes cats have to die.

'How are you today?' He asked the old man.

Jaisax looked up at the boy. If he was surprised to hear him speak, he didn't convey it.

'Same as yesterday and tomorrow,' he said, sipping his whisky.

Kace wasn't too sure if that meant he was good or bad. He hoped it was the former. Jaisax had never caused him any harm. Despite his rugged appearance, he found the old man to be quite sweet at times.

Once, he'd spilt a large amount of his whisky. A simple mistake, knocking it over on his table. Kace had jumped up, offering to clean it, but Jaisax refused to let the boy clean up after him. *My mistake,* he muttered, looking for the tavern's mop.

'How do you know what tomorrow will bring?' Kace asked.

'Because,' Jaisax said, ending the conversation dead in its tracks.

Kace looked back to the ginger ale.

Four, Five, Six.

'What about you?' Jaisax asked. 'How are you?'

Kace smiled and stood up from the ginger ale shelf. His counting could wait.

'I'm hoping tomorrow will be different. Any advice on that?'

Jaisax eyed him, 'And whom do you wish to be tomorrow?'

Kace shrugged weakly. 'Anyone but Kace.'

*

A heavy rainstorm. The splash from unkind cart drivers not avoiding a puddle. The cold wetness that had overcome the King's Town. A storm that had been scheduled but was a shock, nonetheless.

Duxos had been walking through the flower stalls when the skies had opened. He ducked and dived beneath the cover, finally settling himself in the doorway of a tavern.

'Won't let up for quite a while,' a man with a scar said, leaving said-tavern.

Duxos looked at the cheap ale and decided it best to sit a while. He opened the door and stepped in. Empty.

'Hallo,' he called out. On one individual table sat a now empty bottle of whisky and a little glass. He suspected it was where the scarred man once sat.

'One second,' a voice called from the back room.

Duxos smelt the tavern's air. Something felt odd about it. Slowly, he walked towards the bar counter and, for whatever reason, fidgeted with the sharp knife attached to his belt. To feel its cold edge felt comforting.

'Sorry,' the voice said, stepping out and dropping a bag of potatoes, 'what can I get you?'

Duxos looked up at the plump landlady,

'Just an ale, please,' he said, and Flavia went about pulling it from the tall tap.

'Sheltering from the storm?' She asked.

'Aye,' Duxos said, placing a dirty coin on the countertop.

*

Kace lay beneath the very same bar counter, holding his breath.

He waited until he heard the sound of the little man returning the pint glass to the bar top and leaving the tavern.

Kace scrambled out from behind the bottles, giving poor Flavia the biggest fright.

'What are you doing under there?' she cried out.

'Hiding from that man,' Kace replied.

'Why?'

'I don't know,' he said truthfully. For whatever reason, Adiana had knocked him unconscious and told Kace to run from him. He trusted the forest girl and this little mean man was surely not good for his cause. Whatever his cause may be.

The storm had passed, and Kace stepped out into the after rain. Taking the rank smell deep in his nostrils.

Who was he?

After work, hoping for some good luck, Kace took every coin he had (four of them) to the old man in the barber shop and apologetically handed them over.

The barber growled something about him being a wee thief but thanked him for coming back.

'May this be my regular barber?' Kace asked him cheekily.

'If you come back in here,' he said, 'I'm whacking your bottom out with me broom.'

The following days brought a reoccurring anxiety for Kace but, thankfully, the little man didn't return to the tavern. Nor had Kace seen him out and about. Days were passing, and rhythms of life were being formed. Rinse and repeat.

On a warm, bright evening, Kace decided it was time to sneak out to find Elex. The sunset was mellow and kindly introduced him to the night. Kace feigned the want for a walk in the fire-red sunset. Meandering the town's wall until darkness came, and he found a rooftop so close to the wall that scaling it and dropping to the wild other side seemed quite possible.

He quietly climbed atop the closed café roof, stopping just a moment to look at the radiant white moon. Like God was giving him a spotlight, he performed nimble footwork across the tiled roof and towards the wall.

Crouching in the darkness, he waited for nothing in particular, then leapt across to the wall. And, as carefully as he could, dropped down to the grassy ground beneath.

He wandered back towards the town's gates, the spot where he had left Elex, hoping the dog would still be around.

What he would do if he weren't, Kace was unsure. But he had to try.

The town's gate loomed in the distance.

He crept as close as he dared and took the fresh meat he'd stolen from the tavern kitchen and waved it, hoping the scent would catch the dog's nose.

He hunkered by the bush, where something caught his eye. A thing so familiar it stopped him in his tracks.

A royal blue hair bow.

It popped as visibly on the green grass as it did against her green eyes. It was hers, he was so very sure of it. Adiana.

A crunch behind him made him snap back quickly. He thought it was a snake at first. But on closer inspection, he saw it was far too hairy and was moving too happily.

Elex bowed his head like he'd been anticipating Kace's arrival and received the boy's patting.

Kace gave the dog's head a small kiss. He smelt surprisingly fresh (by Elex's standards), and Kace wondered where the dog was washing.

'Good boy,' Kace said as Elex rolled over to show his stomach. It would have been hard, to the outside eye, to tell who was happier to see who. Boy or dog?

Kace showed Elex the hair bow.

'Where is she?'

The dog could not answer. Kace begged his chocolate eyes for one though. Kace looked deep inside them like it was all there.

He followed Elex's eye line to the town's gate. He couldn't be telling him that Adiana had gone in there, could he? If he was, why would she? To look for him?

But why would she have dropped her precious bow? He'd never seen her without it. What would cause her to be so reckless in losing it? He felt a deep hole in the pit of his stomach. He wasn't sure why, but the worry grew like rampant, hungry weeds.

If Adiana was inside the town, how did she get in? With all due respect, she did not look like she belonged in a royal town. And if she had been a stowaway like him, where was she now? Had she been caught by the cart driver? Had she been sent back out to the forest, brought to jail, or worse... He didn't want to think about it.

Elex sniffed the hair bow. Kace's cogs turned.

'Where is she?' he urged. 'Find her.'

Elex sniffed the ground. Kace watched, could the dog's nose lead him the way she'd gone?

'Let's go!' Kace begged, and nose to the ground, Elex led Kace towards the town's gate.

'She went into the town?' Kace said, surer this time. Elex's chocolate eyes had been trying to tell him, after all.

Kace looked at the pacing guard in front of the gate. What remained of his hair flailed in the slight breeze.

Before Kace could gather a plan, Elex started to bark wildly. The balding guard jumped, grabbed his gun and ran towards them.

'Dog!' he shouted as the turret by the gate lit up with resting guards.

Kace's eyes widened. *What are you doing, boy?!* He turned and grabbed the dog by the scruff of his neck and pulled him towards the darkness. But Elex, a genius in his own right, had a plan. He darted off down the ditch and crouched as the guards came closer.

A small window of opportunity. That's all one needs at times if brave enough.

The gate was unmanned now and, while more guards were sure to arrive, for this brief, hectic moment, the gate was open and unwatched.

Kace knew what the dog was thinking. 'Clever, boy!' He patted him, hoping that was a sufficient enough reward for now.

Like there were wheels on his feet, Kace took off, his dog by his side, and bounded towards the gate.

'Stop!' a voice hissed, but it was not the voice of a guard.

Kace and Elex stopped and turned to the unfamiliar voice to see a familiar face.

Kace did a double take, why was this man outside of the town's wall?

'You won't make it,' he hissed, waving Kace back behind a tree. 'Follow me.' He said.

With the sound of boots stomping and opportunity windows slamming shut. Kace, with Elex in pursuit, ducked back into the bushes and followed the man away from the gate.

They walked on quickly. The sound of the guards growing fainter with each step. Kace looked up at the man. In all the times he'd seen him sitting in the tavern, he'd hardly ever seen him standing up. He was tall.

'Jaisax?' Kace whispered.

'Not now, just follow me, boy,' he whispered back, not taking too much notice of the dog that followed. If he had been surprised or repulsed to see the dog, he hadn't shown it.

They continued on, man, boy and dog.

Until finally, the convoy took a turn away from the wall and into the edge of the forest.

Jaisax led them to a well. At least, Kace thought it was well.

But the old man with the scar didn't take a drink from it. Instead, he peered over the edge and down into the thick black.

'Don't look down,' he muttered, climbing onto the ledge. A small, rusted ladder ran all the way down into the darkness.

'We're going down there?!' Kace exclaimed.

Jaisax only nodded and began to reverse his way

down the ladder. The old man was surprisingly agile on his feet. It looked like he did this regularly.

'Stay around here,' Kace said, rubbing Elex's soft ears. The dog seemed to understand a lot, including how a ladder was not built for his four paws.

Elex slunk back to where he was comfortable: the forest.

And Kace took a deep breath and followed Jaisax down the rusty ladder and into the darkness.

A tunnel.

Kace jumped from the last wrung of the ladder and landed on a stone floor. Jaisax told him to trust and led him away from the pinprick of light above them.

It was the type of darkness one can't ever describe. So thick that it was almost dizzying. They carried on into the darkness without so much as even a heavy breath between them.

At no particular point in the darkness, Jaisax stopped abruptly, making Kace break hard too.

'Here,' the man whispered. Kace couldn't see exactly what he was doing, but the man seemed to be patting the rocky ceiling until a deeper *thunk* filled the silence.

It hurt. The brightness of the light.

Jaisax had pushed open a wooden trap door and was pulling himself up into the light. Kace watched his old arms pull him up. He suddenly didn't look all that old. His face was not kind to him.

Kace climbed behind him and blinked hard at the sudden bright light. When the whiteness subsided, he saw he was in a small cellar. Dusty wine bottles and wooden barrels of ale were everywhere.

'Where are we?' Kace mused.

Jaisax smiled. 'You're in my home.'

15.

The tea was a strange one.

Jaisax said it was all he had to offer if the boy wanted a hot drink. The old man went out to the garden and picked a leaf from a tree planted in the garden.
Bringing it back in, he added it to the teapot. It gave a sort of foul liquorice flavour to the beverage.

His house was unexpectantly clean. Kace had anticipated a messy drunk's house.
A hoarder. A slob.

But no, Jaisax kept his house well, and it seemed that everything had its own place. Not a single trinket or piece of jewellery looked astray. And there was jewellery everywhere.

Kace thought back to his mother's bedroom, the chaotic yet somehow organised mess of a bedside table sprawling with rings, necklaces, bracelets and more.

Jaisax, however, had a place for all of it. And it didn't look odd at all.

He must have seen the boy eyeing the pieces.

'Not mine,' he said absently. 'Mostly all belong to my wife.'

Kace thought the word—*wife*—coming from his mouth sounded odd. Like his house being tidy, the fact that he once married seemed queer. Kace's face must have given away his confusion at this.

'Yes, I married,' Jaisax said, anticipating what the boy's mind may be saying. Kace blushed slightly.

It was hard to imagine the man with the bottle of

whisky and the scar having a marriage ceremony. Friends and family gathered. His tribe and his bride all smiling their congratulations and thanks, respectively.

'She died,' he said sadly, looking old again. 'Out in the forest. A snake got her. Wrapped around her leg and sunk its poison into her thigh. We used to both work out there, you see.'

'I'm sorry,' Kace said.

Jaisax shrugged, 'You weren't the snake that did it.'

'Were you there? Did you kill the snake that did it?'

Jaisax handed out a compassionate look, 'No, I didn't. What's the point in two deaths?'

'You're stronger than I'd be if my wife was killed,' Kace said.

The tea's aftertaste was bitter. And in combination with the liquorice, it mixed into a ghastly taste.

'No good?' Jaisax grinned as Kace sipped a second smaller sip.

'It's strong,' is all Kace could say. And with that, Jaisax stood and took the cup from him.

'Do ye like mint?' Jaisax asked.

'I do,' Kace answered.

The next tea Jaisax served was more palatable—a refreshing mint with half a spoon of sugar in it. Kace thanked him, took the cup, glad of its warmth, and sipped.

Jaisax smiled at the boy. It was strange to see him smile this much. Kace found it difficult to place the man's age. He somehow looked both incredibly old yet also strong and agile. His arms, muscular, his core well-defined.

Kace waited for the tea to settle in his stomach before addressing the obvious. With a breath, he said, 'So, that dog—'
But Jaisax just held up his dirty hand and his ungroomed fingers to stop him. 'I'd rather not know,' he said.

Kace fixated on the dirty nails. *How odd*, he thought. Such a clean house yet such dirty nails.
He supposed that the man must spend a lot of time in the forest. Why bother to clean something that'll just be dirty again soon?

'I don't mind them,' Jaisax started, 'you know. Dogs.' He said this like it were a dirty word. 'But I'd rather not know about your business with them.' He cleared his throat, clearly ending the discussion. This was the best reaction that Kace could wish for.
It's okay that you like the dogs, just don't discuss it in my house.
Given the ignorance-fuelled prejudice against them, this was an *okay* reaction.

Kace nodded a thankful understanding, glad of the liberty not to discuss Elex any further. He sipped his minty tea again and planned his next angle of questioning. 'Why do you have a secret tunnel to the forest?'

Jaisax poured a cup of the foul-tasting tea for himself, he splashed a generous shot of whisky in it and sipped.

'I am an amateur gardener,' he said, finally, like it was some kind of inside joke with himself. 'At least, now I am. I used to be professional.'

'What do you mean?' Kace asked.

'I pick and supply fresh plants and flowers in the forest. Well, I used to. I took them through the gate, usually. Gate products, I called them.'

'And what do you pick now? In your amateur gardening era.'

'Tunnel products,' he smirked. 'Things that aren't legal to take through the gate. Plants that are sold beneath the table.'

'I see,' Kace said, seeing the old man in a new light. He was a mischievous old man.

'I work in the cover of darkness,' he said, 'I know every inch of forest around this town. No further than a mile radius from the town, mind you. I'm not crazy enough to wander that deep.' He studied the boy's face after saying this. He must know that Kace came from afar.

'Is that why you only come to the tavern during the day?' Kace asked.

Jaisax nodded and offered the boy a top-up of tea. Kace said, 'Yes, please', and watched the tea fall from the ceramic pot into his glass cup.

'So, tell me, Kace,' Jaisax said, perched now on the sofa's edge, 'who are you? And where did you come from?'

Kace told him mostly everything.

He spoke about Ellon, his father, and his run for the hills with Elex. He opened his mouth and said it all.

Jaisax listened, nodding along. His stare was intense. The type of stare that told Kace he was actually listening.

Kace told him everything except for Adiana. He hadn't had a friend like her, and the thought of outing her to Jaisax felt like breaking some sort of trust between them.

'So, you wandered the forest from Ellon all alone?' Jaisax said in a lull in Kace's story. The boy nodded, yes. Embarrassed to be taking the credit for his survival, but also feeling like he doing the right thing. Wherever Adiana was now, she would surely appreciate her anonymity. She might even need it.

'Tell me about the forest,' Jaisax leaned forward like he was *really* listening now.

'What's there to tell?' Kace shrugged. 'There's snakes, dogs, birds, bees and insects.'

Kace felt a little uneasy all of a sudden. He could swear he saw a glimmer of fear in the old man's eyes.

'It's not that scary if ye know what to look out for,' Kace said, feigning confidence.

'Aye, you're a braver man than I,' Jaisax said.

'You built a tunnel to the forest,' Kace exclaimed, 'it's hardly I that is the brave man here.' Kace liked to call himself a man. Like a smooth chocolate drop, melting around his tongue, it felt nice inside of his mouth.

'My daughter built it,' Jaisax said, picking up a picture of a dusty red-haired girl. 'She was the real genius in the family. Bless her.'

He wondered if Jaisax was setting him up to ask about her or simply lost in his own reverie. He decided to stay off the subject, instead opting to stare at the picture of the man's daughter. She must have been in her early thirties or so in the picture. Kace noted how masculine she dressed; her beige cargo trousers were not too dissimilar to the workmen of Ellon. She was mucky, her hair unkempt and looked oddly familiar at a certain angle.

'Where is she now?' Kace asked, unable to stop himself and find a better way to phrase the question.

Jaisax looked sadly at Kace, and the boy knew not to ask any further questions.

'May I use your tunnel?' Kace asked in the sudden silence. 'To visit Ele—my dog?'

'How can I trust you to keep it a secret?'

'How can I trust *you*?' Kace returned.

'Hm,' Jaisax mused, 'I suppose trust is a two-way street.'

Kace extended his hand and shook the dirty hand belonging to Jaisax. He just hoped that his word was cleaner than the beds of his fingernails.

*

It's funny, she thought. *How enough silence becomes the loudest thing in the land.*

She'd lost count of the days since the jail cell door had slammed shut. The noise of it and the mocking laughs from the guards were the only things she heard, save her own breath, of course. Which sounded small and weak in the dark cell.

For Adiana, this was a test greater than anything the forest could throw at her. Proving further that the most dangerous thing on this planet is man.

She knew what she must do to survive: starve.

The stodgy bread the guards threw her was not nutritious but very fatty. If she could deprive herself of food and grow so thin that she could slide out of the chains and into the block hole in her cell where she was expected to do her business, there must be a way out down there. The stone hole that could hardly be called a toilet was about the size of a small well. It would be impossible for a healthy large man or even a woman to get down through the tunnel, but with her little size and ever-shrinking body mass, surely she could fit down.

It must lead somewhere. It would be grim. Far from a luxurious way to escape, but she knew it *would* be hard to escape regardless. And this is what hard looked like.

The guards through a hard loaf at her. Food for the two days. She picked at it, tearing it into small pieces and stuffed it in the wall cracks around her.

In the deadly silence of the night, rats nibbled on the bread. The odd one broke free of the wall and scurried over her feet.

This is what hard looks like.

*

Duxos stuck his little finger into the hot liquid wax. Pulling it out, it hardened around his fingertip like a cast.

A week in the King's town and no sight of the boy. Perhaps he was dead. Or worse, back out in the forest. If he was, the longer he stayed in the town, the colder the trail on him would get. It would get so cold that not even a skilled tracker like Duxos could locate him. And he was not about to look inept.

He picked at the hard wax. Where was he? Where was Kace?

The tavern he sat in was beginning to get loud. The hum of the early evening quickly escalated to a cacophony of white noise. The odd piercing laugh of a drunk cut through the continuous sound like the sharp thing it was.

'You new to the town?' a man with a hood too big said to Duxos.

'A passerby. A journalist,' Duxos lied, sipping his drink.

'Aye, here's to you. Welcome.' The hooded man drank. 'How long do you expect to be here for?'

'What is with the questioning?'

'Well, I imagine someone has paid you a pretty penny to be here? Shame to be wasting your time drinking in a pub.'

Duxos recognised the accent suddenly. He sighed and moved closer to the man.

'So you reckon he's in this town, do you?' Sander said as Duxos moved closer. The two men sitting side by side on the bar stool looked like quite the comical sight. A man too big for the stool and a man whose feet couldn't reach the floor. They were an odd pair.

'I should have sent a message.'

'Yes, you should have.'

'But I believe your son may well be here, yes.'

'You reckon he's at the bottom of that ale glass?' Sander mocked. Duxos reddened and signalled the barmaid for two more. He supposed he owed his client a drink. If not his son and the dog, he could at least get him an ale.

'I've found myself out of my comfort zone, not being in the forest,' Duxos admitted.

Sander's face gave nothing away, a stoic man striking a stoic pose.

'But I will not stop looking for him.' Duxos's thin finger pressed into the bar counter to drill the point home. 'Sander, I promise I'll find him.'

'Your word means nothing anymore.'

Sander drank from the fresh ale. He gulped half of the pint in three large mouthfuls and stood.

'Don't make me come find you again.' Sander roughly grabbed the little man's shirt collar, 'I'll be staying in the town until you find him.'

Duxos nodded.

'And if I find him before you do,' Sander hissed, 'I'm getting my money back.'

The other half of his ale was still cold and bubbling on the bar counter.

'Thanks for the drink,' Sander said, walking away.

Duxos put down two coins on the bar counter and went out to search for the boy.

*

Nearly thin enough, she thought.

The bones on her wrist were more visible than when she'd started her stint in jail.

Nearly time to leave this wretched place. Nearly.

A guard started to bang on her jail cell.

'Ye are as thin as a broom,' he remarked, throwing two loaves of bread at the girl.

'I want to see you eat them both. Ye are not to starve yourself in here.'

'I'm not hungry,' Adiana whispered to him.

'How can ye not be hungry?' He laughed loudly. 'Maybe ye just don't like bread.' He smirked and, in some beautifully cruel way, she knew she was to be tested further.

The second guard came in with a tray of freshly cooked chicken. Her stomach clawed for it. How good it smelt.

'Eat,' the guard said, placing the tray in front of Adiana and leaving.

How truly good the chicken smelt...

Alone now, the smell seemed to seep into every nook and cranny of the tiny stone cell. The rats, who normally stayed quiet during the day, were scurrying frantically in the direction of the scent.

She couldn't.

She mustn't.

One bite wouldn't hurt.

She crawled over to the hot meat and, with her thin fingers and thin hands, ripped at the dead animal and scoffed it into her mouth. How truly good the chicken tasted.

Tomorrow her body wouldn't look any different. One feed will not make a person fat. But she was scared to try now. She'd broken her willpower—and when one breaks that once, how easy it is to break over and over.

The following morning, the bread came in, and she was desperate to capture the euphoria of the previous day's chicken. So she did, what's the point? She'd already broken her fast once.

Hope is a funny thing, she thought as the stodgy bread expanded in her wilting stomach. Hope is single-handedly the most powerful thing a person can have, yet also the most fragile.

A simple dead chicken.

Some flour, water and a pinch of yeast.

All thieves of hope.

She lay, her stomach full of chicken and bread. What chance did she have in fitting down that pipe now? Her hope lay shattered amongst the bread crumbs and chicken bones. As ugly as them too.

16.

Kace used the tunnel twice a day for three days. Bringing food to Elex, taking walks with him, and bathing in the clear air. All activities of such pleasure. The slow breeze occasionally gave him sharp goosebumps. He looked like a little berry bush. Ready to pick.

On the fourth day, Jaisax stepped from his study and handed Kace a little sewn bag of crushed dried out leaves and asked him to bring it to the other side of the town.

'Repayment for letting you use my tunnel,' Jaisax said stiffly. 'The long walk isn't good for me.'

And so Kace made his way across to the far side of the town's wall. The walk ached even his young knees. On one of the streets, he was sure that he saw his father. A glimpse of a man as meaty as Sander flashed past. Alas, it could not be his father. He knew it was implausible. He shook the thought free of his head and carried on.

The woman he met took the bag from him and handed over a bundle of notes in return. It was the most amount of money he'd ever seen.

'Get this back to J,' she said. The woman was sketchy-looking, Kace thought. She had wispy white hair that was ungroomed, and she was so thin that he thought of her as having some sort of medical condition. She sniffed the air like a dog and scurried back to her small apartment door.

Kace had never seen so much money. Actual notes of it. Only the rich have notes. But this woman did not appear rich. Her apartment looked unassuming and sat beneath a tall façade of other apartments.

A man with a cigarette hanging floppy from his mouth stood on the tallest balcony and watched Kace like a bird preparing to swoop down to its prey.

The trips from Jaisax to the apartments became more frequent. It was like clockwork, every evening after he'd returned from playing with Elex in the forest. Bathing in the light amongst the trees, Jaisax would hand him the bag of dry leaves and send him to the apartments.

Then Jaisax began to pay him.

The first was just a simple coin. But then, a note.

Kace had never had a note to his name. He didn't want to spend it. He just wanted to have a note for a while. He lay it gently in the jacket of a hardback book and tucked it into the bookshelf away from the tax man and the dirty hands that cleaned the inn rooms twice a week. It's not that he didn't trust them as such, but it was true that Flavia tended to hire the less favourable amongst society for those jobs that didn't involve talking to the public. Hence perhaps, why a scraggly, homeless Kace had wormed his way in.

It's like the note was breathing.

The air in his bedroom was pulsating around where he knew he had it kept. How good would it be to have two of them? Kace mused.

It was approaching night, and the temptation was all too real. Money was sure to come again. If he kept up the role as Jaisax's courier, surely there would be more notes to come. So what if he lost just this one note?

He snatched the crisp note from inside the book and fell out of his inn bedroom, towards a place that was so inviting: the largest gambling house in all the land.

A place where the king himself is often found.

'Ye have been away a lot of late,' Flavia called as Kace made his way across the tavern floor to the door.

'I'm a busy man,' Kace said.

'Is that so? Busy man making coin?'

If only she knew, he thought, 'I am a poor man still.'

'I'd have to start charging more for the room if you are making more.'

'No, I am not.' The boy lied, making a swift exit.

That first gambling win in Ellon, way back, had been a high Kace had yearned for ever since. Even just to have a small glimpse of it. A flicker. A single little ember of it.

He walked through the blackening night, the royal blue sky above the regal town looking down and lighting his way. The small dots. Hard to believe that they were stars all the way up there.

He looked up. *Is this it? Is this my life?*

He wondered if he had *made it* whatever that might mean. He thought it amusing that he couldn't quite tell if he was in the depths of the worst, or the height of the high. They looked quite similar at that moment.

And so he entered the gambling house with its bright lights and promises to win. Cash and carry. The buzz of winners and losers drinking away their grasp on reality. The host looked at Kace funny but, after proving he could pay to play, he was let in.

'One full on black, please,' Kace said after overhearing the language. A full is a note. Noted.

The worker nodded and took Kace's note, clipping it beneath a spring in a wooden box. He spun the wheel, throwing in the ball at random.

It bounced like a thick rabbit, hopping from segment to segment. White to black. White to black. Black. Black. White. Black. White. White.

Black.

Kace smiled, his winnings were double his stake. Two notes were handed over to him. He stood and walked to the next table.

'Two full to play,' the worker said, dealing a row of cards out.

Kace handed over the two notes. It wasn't real money, it was just stupid winnings. Money that he didn't have before.

He'd never played the card game before, but he learnt fast. Winning the first and losing the second.

He was fuzzy from the constant trays of alcohol being delivered to him. From where he didn't know, but he was glad of them. Little flutes of confidence boosters.

Next bet, and the next until.

He reached into his pocket for coins. Empty.

'Pay to play,' the table's worker, a fat man with a moustache, chirped.

'Wait,' Kace said, searching his pockets and satchel. Surely there was more money in here? He had won more than he lost, surely?

The moustache man huffed and turned to the next

punter, 'I'll deal ye in.'

Kace hadn't a coin left. The building must have had eyes as the drinks stopped coming then.

He stumbled his way towards the exit.

'I'll spot you a coin,' a voice said.

Kace turned to see the little man leant against a pole. His smirk was a proud one.

'Play with me, Kace,' the little man said, still smirking.

Curiosity took his hand and led him astray, and Kace nodded to play. The pair silently made their way to a table. A fleeting thought arrived and went. To ask the man his name, or not? Kace opted for silence. It felt a whole lot less revealing.

'I'm paying in for him,' Duxos declared to the worker, who nodded and went about fixing their deck of cards.

'Who are you?' Kace asked.

'A man with a job.'

'And what's your job?'

'Two full, one each,' Duxos said aloud, smiling as he placed the notes down.

And they were up and playing. They were in the game. Equals for just one moment. Not prey and hunter, but two in competition only.

Duxos played his first hand. Kace's drunk eyes spun, trying their best to focus on his cards. The numbers were fuzzy. The icons indecipherable.

'If I win,' Duxos mused quietly, 'you tell me where the dog is.'

'And if *I* win?' Kace said with a sudden wave of nausea.

'I give you a head start.' Duxos grinned. His teeth were a shade of yellow that made Kace feel even more unwell. He locked into the little man's teeth and imagined tiny flies zipping around them like they do in the cow fields. The staining, from many bloody meals, looked odd in the royal town's gambling house. Duxos's smart suit, a contrast of great proportions.

At first glance, Kace's hand appeared to be weak. He felt that playing it would lead to trouble, so he chose to stick and hold, and drew a new card from the dealer. Duxos had a sly smile on his face as he laid down a strong hand.

'You know, Kace, little boys who run towards the light get blinded.'

'The light is beautiful though,' Kace whispered, sticking to his cards for a second time.

Duxos huffed, 'It's an illusion. Shade is comfortingly beautiful.'

'I disagree.' Kace laid down his hand. Two extras picked, but he needed to play. Duxos eyed the cards as they rested on the velvet table-top, grinning when he saw the poor hand. Kace's eyes found a small candle burning across the room. It reminded him of the small fire his father would light at home. He pictured a mini version of his father poking it, the thought in his fuzzy head made him laugh. Duxos eyed him like he was a mad boy.

'Fresh deal,' the worker said, dealing out two piles.

When Kace picked up the slippery cards, he thought back to a conversation his father had with him once. *Your cards are your cards, play them and ye might win. Don't, and you'll lose for sure.*

The context escaped him. What they had been talking about Kace did not know. But the line had dug itself a home deep within his brain.

He looked at his hand, deadpan. The cards laughed either at or with him, he wasn't sure.

Duxos laid down his hand, average at best.

Then Kace laid down his.

The dealer nodded. Kace smiled, and Duxos didn't.

'Full to the boy,' the worker said, pushing the winnings over to Kace. 'In or cash out?'

Kace's head spun. 'I'm out.'

'He's out,' and the worker, suddenly uninterested, went about collecting the cards and preparing for the couple that sat waiting to play next.

'I'll be off.' Kace jumped from the bar stool.

'Run fast, boy,' Duxos snarled, 'I'm coming.'

Kace made a quick pace. With a confident stride, he dismissed his perpetual restlessness. A sense of home had eluded him thus far, but he could only continue and hope for a place to rest longer.

The King's Town was a shallow place. He thought it was shining, but really, it was only a reflection.

At the gambling house door, Kace stopped for a moment and took in the last of the shiny room. Drinking what was once a hopeful liquid. He spat it out and carried on out into the night.

'The girl was found in the forest.'

The sentence cut through the night air and drilled itself into Kace's ears.

He spun to the two men, sitting smoking by the door. Two large guards gossiped in a hushed voice.

'Sorry,' Kace said, startling the men, 'what did you say about a girl found in the forest?'

The guards erected themselves, embarrassed at having been caught in the act of a babbling tongue.

'Nothin' you need worry about,' one of them said, dismissing the small boy in his oversized suit.

As Kace was pushed away, he felt a violent sickness in his stomach. Adiana? And what did they mean by *found?* Dead? Alive?

He rushed back to the inn and began to pack his rucksack. Flavia darkened his bedroom doorway.

'I wondered when ye would run off,' she said, like she'd seen it all before.

'It's not safe for me here anymore,' Kace said sorrowfully.

'Is that so? Well, be gone.' Flavia wrung the tea towel in her hands. 'Hope to see ye again.'

Kace smiled at her back and let her walk away. 'Thank you,' he called after her, but he was unsure if she heard him.

She was gone. Moving stealthily like a phantom into the shadows of the evening.

17.

A crown is a silly thing.

A pompous hat that tells the world you were born into royalty and inherently better than everyone. But it all means very little when God steals your final breath.

Of all the nights for the king to die, this night was not ideal for Kace, who found himself eaten by the mob of mourners flooding the town's streets.

'What's going on?' Kace asked a group outside of the tavern.

'The king has died, we think. We're all to go to the tower.'

Kace climbed a small stone wall and looked over the sea of bowed heads, slowly shuffling to the tower. 'Everyone and their mothers to the tower to pay their respects,' one of the king's guards shouted along the street. Kace watched the sea trundle forwards slowly.

Flavia stepped out of the tavern. 'Some divine thing is telling you to stay,' she uttered to Kace. The boy could only walk forwards with the crowd.

His feet, like two blocks of concrete, shuffled forward in the thick crowd. The townspeople's shoulders bumped against him roughly, a silent scrum of sorts. His eyes scanned the bowed heads. Where was the little man?

The King's men led the town to the courtyard beneath the tower.

Quite the sight, Kace thought, looking at the many people—tall and small, man, woman and child—all silently standing like the most sombre of performers was due to appear.

Flavia, slower, had fallen back behind, and Kace had found himself deep in the thickest part of the crowd. *The open air is too exposed. Stay tucked in*, he thought.

The King's consort stepped out onto the balcony of the tower. She pinned a large notice that read;

The King died peacefully this morning.

The message, hushed and slow in a whisper, spread through the crowd like a virus.

She stepped back inside the tower, and the people awaited whatever was to come.

Kace continued to scan. The little man must be somewhere about. Everyone was here. All the late King's guards, the shopkeepers, the doctors, the farmers, the drunks, and even the prisoners.

The prisoners.

Kace felt his heart drop. His eyes combed along the chain-linked prisoners, who stood on the far side of the courtyard, looking sorry for themselves.

And there she was.

The funniest looking thing next to the bearded, burly criminals.

The small, scruffy Adiana. With the chains too big for her and the small twigs from the forest still stuck in her long hair.

From the royal balcony shouted a man, 'Please all stand for the late King's vicar!'

A bishop stepped onto the balcony and began to shout a prayer down to the town below.

Kace dropped to his hands and knees and crawled fast. He aimed for the long line of prisoners. The people above him tutted.

Silly child.

He sped out beneath the grieving legs and sat still behind a plant pot. A few people glanced, he feigned sorrow for the king's death, and they looked away to give him the privacy they thought he craved.

The row of prisoners was flanked by armed guards. He wasn't all too sure what he would do next, but God Himself gave up the answer.

'And now we pray!' The vicar shouted, and the crowd dipped their heads and closed their eyes. The prison guards removed their hats and, to Kace's delight, also closed their eyes.

Now or never, Kace.

Silently, like walking across a frozen lake, he tiptoed towards the prisoners and, with a water-like fluidity, he reached for Adiana's bowed head and covered her mouth with his hand.

Every breath felt loud in the deathly quiet courtyard. His heart beat loudly in his throat and behind his ears. The closest guard sniffed a slight sniff, freezing Kace to the spot, then returned to whatever he was thinking about.

Kace slipped the chain off of Adiana's thin wrist. He picked at the ankle ones. Adiana, seeing who he was now, tried the same.

The rattle of the chain caused the other prisoners to stir. But, after seeing what was happening, they simply looked back down. Kace felt a torn sense of gratitude for the men who most likely had committed all sorts of heinous crimes.

She slipped out with relative ease. Her starved body was far smaller than anything the chains were used to holding.

Kace and Adiana scurried on their hands and knees.

'Amen!' shouted the bishop over the crowd. The heads belonging to the townspeople came up again.

Behind them, there was a commotion.

The sniffing guard must have looked at his prisoners straight away.

But it didn't matter to Kace and Adiana, for they were up off of their hands and knees and running away from the tower.

'Where are we going to go?' Adiana said.

'Trust me,' and Kace smiled, feeling free for the first time in days. They were born to run, these two.

They ran all the way to a place Kace was beginning to know well.

'What was that place?' Adiana exclaimed as they climbed up to the grassy freedom of the forest.

'A friend's tunnel,' Kace smirked, and the two ran back into the darkness of the forest together.

*

He had watched it all. Stuck on a side street by the tower, unable to move. When the bishop called the prayer, the sea of eyes dropped, except for a pair he knew all too well. His son's eyes.

Sander watched as his son dropped to the floor and resurfaced like a drunk mole on the other side of the courtyard, freeing a girl from the chain and making their way out of the crowd.

Hours later, when the crowd was finally dispersing, he found Duxos in a nearby tavern and grabbed him by his collar.

'You let him get away!'

And Sander found himself beating Duxos until the guards came and took Sander to a cell in the tower that a small, bushy-haired girl had recently occupied.

*

Behind them came the sound of iron gates opening and horse's hooves clopping. The unmistakable sound of a chase. So they ran until the sounds disappeared and the trail behind them cooled.

'I think we lost them,' Kace said weakly between breaths. The weeks spent in the King's Town had made him unfit. Flavia's food and ale had been delicious but fattening. Creamy sauces and thick gloopy pies caused him difficulty in keeping up with Adiana, as light-footed as ever, she skimmed along the forest floor.

Hunger was a familiar foe to Adiana, and the weeks locked away didn't diminish her energy but instead gave her the sharpness one can only get from the need to eat. Primal.

'Keep up,' she quipped back to the panting Kace,

smiling as she did, 'you've put on weight. You're fat.'

'No need to be so straight with me. There are such things as manners,' Kace panted.

She smirked again, showing him the white teeth that surprised him each time she smiled. How does she keep them so clean, especially in jail?

Amazingly, somehow, they'd gotten even more white. Kace stared at them dumbly for a long moment.

'Where do we go?' Adiana asked in a small voice that broke Kace from his reverie. It was a voice that might even be mistaken for fear. Kace felt a chill at the thought of her, of all people, being afraid in the forest.

'I…' Kace ruminated for a moment, before shaking his head, 'I don't know.'

'You don't know? But doesn't he always have a plan?'

'I don't know where to go, Adiana. I really don't. I suppose all I've ever wanted to do is run and find, but I'm just so very tired of running.'

'Then why don't you stop?'

'Because I'm scared. I'm scared of staying still. It brings out the terrors. It makes…' Kace stopped at the sudden impact of the feeling.

Adiana pressed herself against him.

She hugged him. Long and hard, and then squeezed him tight.

'You looked like you needed that,' she said, pulling back out of the embrace. 'I haven't had a hug in a long time, you know.' She said, shyly.

'Me neither,' he said quietly.

'It was nice.'

'It was.'

Kace looked out to the deep dark forest and, with pursed lips, blew a long hard whistle.

They waited until the nearby bushes shook and the sound of paws breaking sticks filled the silence. Elex's tail wagged hard at the sight of the boy and the girl.

'Hi, boy,' Kace said, rubbing between his ears and down his face. The dog playfully nibbled on Kace's hand. He could easily tear it off if he desired. But of course, he didn't.

Adiana gave the dog a quick pat on the ribs and started to pick at his fur. Her fingers found an insect in his thickening coat, 'He's got creepy crawlies in his fur.'

Kace picked at the little angry insects now, too, 'are they dangerous?' He asked.

'Sometimes they can carry diseases,' Adiana said, 'but that's rare, don't worry. We should pick them off, though.'

'He's scratching,' Kace said concerned as the dog's back paw scratched at no area in particular.

'I'd be scratching too if I had a lot of insects crawling all over me.' Adiana huffed.

'Let's find a river,' Kace said, standing and helping Adiana up off of the ground.

The three; the boy, the girl and the dog made their way down the hill towards the softer ground. Stopping ever so often to prod the grass, 'it's getting softer. There's water somewhere,' Adiana said.

'Oh, do stop scratching, Elex, it'll only make it

worse.' Kace pleaded with the dog that could not understand him.

When they finally found the lagoon, their mouths dropped open. The fall of a loud waterfall bubbled and frothed in the otherwise clear water.

'This river must run all the way into the King's Town. This water is royal.' Kace said, amazed at the glass-like water.

There was a slight, chilling spray on them as the water cascaded.

'I hope they enjoy insects in their water,' Adiana said as Elex jumped in, desperate to drown the crawlers in his fur.

Kace and Adiana sat down on the bank of the lagoon as they watched the dog paddling about, relieving himself from the itches.

'It's beautiful here,' Adiana said.

'Do you want to jump in?' Kace asked with a sudden childlike smirk.

'Sure,' Adiana jumped up, and they headed for a tower of rocks by the deepest part. Nature's diving board.

'Together?' Kace asked, but when he turned he saw that his friend was already plummeting. She crashed through the surface of the water. Kace muttered, 'Or not,' to himself and jumped too.

The feeling of the cold water wrapped around him like a parcel. He felt alive again. But not in the cliché way of life or death, a slumber terminating. No, the cold jolted his euphoria to life again. Really living.

He surfaced and, whilst treading the water, started

to laugh deep in his belly. A massive laugh, an infectious laugh that spread and sickened Adiana too.

Elex, doggy paddled over to them, the noise of their glee disguised as a treat.

'Again?' Kace cheered, pulling himself from the water and climbing back onto the rocks. He jumped again, the air, the water, the impact, all individual little injections of happiness. Intoxicating little things too.

Afterwards, they lay back on the grassy bank, with Elex shaking himself free of the now-dead insects. He lay, satisfied and attempted to dry his fur.

They dried in the sun efficiently and even started to turn a pinky red. But they couldn't care less. It was all too nice. Adiana picked at some blades of grass. Throwing them around with little regard.

'What do you want?' She whispered to the boy.

'I want a home,' he said with a clarity as clear as the water by their feet.

'You want *your* home, or you want *a* home?' She asked like it were the most logical of questions.

'I want *a* home.' He replied.

Adiana turned back up towards the fire in the sky, absorbing its heat, 'I could be your home.'

'You can't *be* a home.'

'Home is the people, not the place,' Adiana said.

*

In a jail cell in the King's town, Sander sat with a tear in his eye.

A watery tear. A really wet one. His eyes stung and puffed from it.

One of the guards opened the door and grabbed him roughly, bringing him out by chains to the court.

All rise, the guards shouted as the judge entered and sat.

'Sander Di Comb, you are here on assault charges. A Mr Duxos Cassvange, who remains in hospital following your senseless attack. How do you plead?'

Sander stood, 'guilty.'

'Sander Di Comb, as your crimes were committed here in the late King's town, you will be jailed within these city walls upon further investigations. Given your lack of resources in this town, your invalid pass to travel, and your previous drunk and disorderly offences in Ellon, you will be transferred to a maximum-security prison. I sentence you twenty years behind bars.'

Sander felt like he'd swallowed a stone, 'your honour, I was only trying to find my son.'

'Mr Di Comb, I'm sorry. Our town does not tolerate delinquent outsiders. You are dismissed.'

There was no trial.
No plea.
No evidence was given.

Sander was simply handed his sentence and was escorted from the court. Things were unfair in the King's town if one was an outsider.

Alone in his cell, the single wet tear from before had birthed a litter of tears. He silently sobbed in his cell, longing to start all over again.

18.

'Let go, Kace.'

'No, Da, I can't.'

'I'm here. Just try.'

'What if I drown, Da?'

'I wouldn't let that happen.'

Kace's hands released their grip.

The small fishing boat they bobbed in,

Kace's safety, slipped from him.

'I'm swimming!'

'You're swimming!' Sander cried out.

'Kace, boy, you're swimming! I'm so proud!'

But something weird happened then.

'Da, where are you going?' Kace asked weakly.

But his Da did not hear,

as the boat bobbed away from him.

It soon became just a brown dot.

And death pulled him beneath the surface.

He awoke sweating, the transparent liquid, like icing on his forehead.

Adiana was next to him, sitting upright, holding his hand. On his other side, Elex lay with a concerned look on his fleecy face. He gave the boy's other hand a small lick.

'Nightmare?' Adiana asked.

'Kind of,' Kace flushed a crimson red, 'I'm fine, though.' He cleared his throat.

'You don't have to be so brave, Kace. You can tell me about your demons. That's what friends are for. Don't you know?'

'I never had friends growing up.' Kace admitted.

'Not one friend?'

'One maybe. Wyeth, but only because I saw him every day in the bakery.'

'Did he like bread?'

'He worked there, he was the baker's son.'

Kace slowly extracted his hand from Adiana's now sticky hands. He wiped his forehead with some torn fabric from his top. The forest was already beginning to take its toll on his once neat clothes.

'I was home-schooled. My parents. They had a lot of worries.'

'Had?' Adiana asked.

'I guess my Da still does. Ma, though, she's been relieved of hers.' Kace began to feel his eyes sting. 'At least, I hope she has. That's all a person deserves in the afterlife. The chance to be calm.'

'I am sure that she is,' Adiana smiled, 'You know, Kace, I've never really had friends either. To be honest. I've never, not once, ever have I had a *best* friend.'

'I could be your best friend,' Kace said timidly.

'What does that entail?'

'I don't really know, but, um, we can figure it out together.'

'The bread boy won't be too disappointed, will he?'

'I don't imagine I'll ever see him again, you see.'

'Oh,' Adiana mused, 'doesn't seem like too best a friend if you never end up seeing him again.'

'I guess,' Kace said, smiling at his newly appointed

best friend.

'Thank you,' she said, 'for saving me from jail.'

'You'd do the same for me.'

'I would,' she said, sure of herself.

'I suppose,' Kace started, 'that's what it is to be a best friend.'

'I think I like it already,' Adiana said, standing now, 'we should keep moving.'

'Where are we going?' Kace asked.

'We don't know,' Adiana called back to him, 'but we'll get nowhere if we stay still.'

Kace, Adiana, and Elex were walking, possibly without realizing it, towards Ellon and its neighbouring forest. Adiana knew the area so well, and each step closer to the familiar felt like a relief for them both. For better or worse, nostalgia is a potent painkiller.

'It feels like a lifetime ago when I ran out of Ellon and into the forest.' Kace said. Adiana considered this, and they carried on walking.

'Do you ever try to find her?' Kace found himself asking in the silence.

'Who?'

'Your Ma,' Kace said.

Adiana stopped, 'she's sure to be dead, Kace. There's nothing to find. The birds and the maggots have made a meal of her by now.'

Kace was repulsed at her brash nature, he supposed death is not an odd thing when living in the harsh forest.

'Do you not wander these forests wondering?'

Kace asked, curiously.

'Quite the opposite,' Adiana sighed gently, 'being in the forest connects me to her. Reminds me of what she once was. Her and the forest, are not two separate entities. Mother nature and she are the same people. At least in my head they are and that brings me great comfort.'

'I don't understand,' Kace admitted, making Adiana smile.

'Are you hungry?'

'I'm always hungry,' Kace said.

With the elegant smoothness of a dancer, she tip-toed over to a tree and picked from its lowest branch, a dull brown shell-like thing.

'What is it?' Kace asked as Adiana brought it over to him.

'It's a piece of fruit.'

'I've never seen it before.'

'It doesn't last more than a few hours after being picked,' Adiana explained, 'only those who are friends with the forest know what it's like.'

Kace watched as she impressively twisted the brown shell open, revealing a white, creamy inside.

'Try it,' she said, handing him half of the fruit.

Kace took his index finger and scooped some out. It was the consistency of warmed butter. A soft but also textured cream. Kace had never tasted anything like it. It was milky sweet as well as well-balanced and nutty.

'These are amazing,' he said, scooping more and offering some to Elex, 'try this!'

The dog took the dollop of the meaty fruit from the boy's fingers and ate it joyfully. Kace ate his portion of the fruit in just a few moments. Hardly savouring it, but enjoying it, nonetheless.

'It's full of energy and will keep ye full for hours,' Adiana said, 'it's a rare tree, though. The people from the King's Town come out and chop them down.'

'Why would they do that?' Kace exclaimed, 'Haven't they tried some?'

'I told you. It can't be kept fresh, so there's no coin to be made from them.'

'We could figure out how to keep them fresh! Sell them and become rich!'

Adiana laughed, 'Oh, Kace, you're such a dreamer. There's no way to keep them fresh, smarter people than us have tried.'

'There must be a way?'

'Why must there be? Can't something just live and die beautifully in the forest? Why *must* something be exploited for coin?'

'I guess I am just an optimist,' Kace said quietly.

'You're trying to live a million lives in your only one. Kace, take a moment and breathe in the forest air.'

He did.

'This,' she continued, 'is all that is real now.'

They continued on, both breathing the forest in like it was the last time they'd have oxygen.

When they found a place to settle for the night, Kace told her he needed a moment alone.

'Are you ok?' She asked, and he smiled a reassurance.

He stood at the edge of a cliff and gazed at the vast

expanse of trees, yearning for something more. What exactly that was, he didn't know. He felt scared at the thought of never having that answer. Perhaps, he was forever just destined to be confused. There might never be a moment of sudden clarity. Maybe life is just wandering the forest, confused, until something kills you.

Nearby, Adiana hid behind some bushes, uncertain of how to help. Though she couldn't come up with an answer, she decided it best to keep a watchful eye on him. She knew that even by doing the bare minimum, she was still doing something. And sometimes, just something is enough.

The next morning, Kace, Adiana, and Elex approached Ellon and encountered hunters with similar accents to Kace.

They hid behind a bush as the two men with two guns each passed by, discussing some sort of storm. The hunters then headed back towards Ellon, and behind them, Kace noticed a dark grey cloud in the distance, confirming the storm's approach.

'We should try to get to my cave today,' Adiana said, to fill the need for a plan.

But Kace had an idea. And he told her such.

'What if we get caught?' She asked, concerned.

'Has that ever stopped us before?' Kace smiled.

'And you're sure it's empty?'

'As sure as anything.'

They made their way south, around the perimeter of Ellon's boundary. As they passed the playing fields,

Kace felt a pang of homesickness for a place he hated so much.

The forbidden house loomed tall. The chimney stacks and tiled roof were just about visible in the distance.

'How do we get in?' Adiana asked.

'Climb, of course.'

The dark cloud was above them now. The air had a stale pre-storm mugginess to it. Like the rain was awaiting its cue in the wings.

They broke into the empty house, the roof if you could even call it that, was enough to keep the first few fat drops off of them.

The first time he came here, the night he ran from Ellon, it had been a disappointment. But here and now, with Adiana and Elex, it felt more like how he'd imagined it to be. The same house that was once a disappointment had transformed itself into a beacon of hope again. He thought about how Adiana might just have been right when she said it's the people that make a house a home.

The rain was thick and heavy, so they wandered further into the house. The entrance hall, kitchen and dining room, all with leaky, exposed roofs, were not providing much refuge.

But down the back of the house, a small snuggery room, with piles of mouldy books, still wore its hat.
The roof above them felt like a simple luxury. A relief from the wet house. They settled down, and tiredness took them. It's an odd thing waking up both inside and out.

Kace took a moment to remember where he was. A small snuggery in the forbidden house. He looked all around. Adiana was still asleep, while Elex was awake and sat loyally by the door.

Kace wondered if the dog had slept at all, or if he was taking it upon himself to guard his humans. Kace patted the floor for the dog to come and join him. He did, and as soon as the furry head rested beside Kace, the guard dog had fallen asleep. Giving way to day watch.

Outside the snuggery, from the kitchen, a bird's nest filled with a little feathery choir sang a morning song.

The storm hadn't been too bad by the looks of things, the wind and rain had left little damage.

Kace stood and wandered out into the open kitchen and beyond to the first of three bedrooms.

He wondered who had lived here, once upon a time, and why so far from Ellon itself. The only thing of note was the farm nearby. He wondered if the people who had lived here had originally been farmers. Milking cows or similar.

By the bed, he picked up a small painting of a little boy. He couldn't have been very old at all, just a wee lad, smiling in the garden. With age, the canvas had faded, and Kace stared at the little boy, wondering who he was.

On the other side of the bed, sat an equally faded painting. Propped up against the wall, as if it had fallen one night in a storm.
The portrait was of a young happy couple smiling beneath a shower of flowers.

He stared at it for a long moment before his breath fell from his lungs.

It had taken him a moment to recognise them as he

had never seen them that happy. But there, on a beach, in a white dress and a smart groom's suit, stood his parents.

19.

Kace wandered through the entire forbidden house, unafraid. He peeled back the curtains to every room. Looked at every detail more closely. The rotting dining room table had the proud initials S.D.C. carved on its belly.

'My Da always carves his initials into every piece of furniture he makes,' Kace explained to Adiana, who wandered with him like an obedient plus one.

Elex, somehow, also seemed to feel the history of the place. He sniffed each room curiously, like he, too, was discovering its secret past.

Below the master bed, Kace found a small leather-bound book, which remained moderately intact. It appeared to be a small diary. The first few pages were hardened by rain and barely legible. Kace tore open the pages, he could just about make out familiar handwriting. The handwriting that used to help him with his homework. His mother's handwriting.

Saturday, May 31st

Today is the first sign of summer, the birds are tweeting, and there is heat in the sun. I imagine that I will take a stroll to the farm for some milk and then into the town for supper supplies. Perchance we could eat outside, for it appears to stay warm until the sun sets these days. I shall ask Sander when he returns from work if he should care to enjoy the outside air. For isn't that why we moved here? To live so close to the forest and breath its life fully. I must go for the little one is needing my attention.

Love always... B 193

Kace turned the page to see a blank one staring back at him. He found his tears returning and shielded his face from Adiana.

'It's ok to cry,' she said gently.

'Do you ever find yourself grieving for a family you never had?' Kace asked.

Adiana stepped towards him and pulled him into a hug. 'Do you even need to ask me that, Kace?'

And they cried for a moment. Allowing themselves to grieve for what was never theirs.

In the back garden, Kace found the garden to be like a set of a tragic play. Abandoned by the actors and its audience.

The decking had a mouldy mug of ale sitting on it. Presumably, where Sander had sat on that fateful evening.

In the centre stage, was what remained of the picnic Brithe had set up many years ago. A small rotting table, a tablecloth, a smashed plate. It was as if time had frozen still, and the worst moment for the new parents had been kept eternal in a painting. A horrid painting.

Kace watched as Elex sniffed about the garden, stopping at the table and looking towards the boy.

He felt like he was standing in the moment. Seeing what his parents saw all those years ago.

He felt an ugly anger boil up from deep within. He strode forward to Elex and shouted as loud as he could.

'Get out, mutt! Go!'

Elex, startled, whimpered and retreated back.

'You ruined my family! You're all murderers!' He shouted at the dog. Whose ears were flopping back sadly.

Adiana ran from the decking as if playing the role of Sander all those years ago.

'Kace, please!' She begged as the boy began to push the dog away into the garden's overgrown bushes.

'Leave me alone!' He cried out, dropping to his knees, helplessly.

The dog's big brown eyes stared at Kace, feeling sorry for himself.

'Go!' Kace screamed, and the dog, with his tail between his legs, slunk off into the bushes and over the garden wall. Giving one last look at the pleading boy.

Elex would do whatever his human wanted him to do, even if that meant leaving.

The hours turned into days, and the days into weeks. Kace and Adiana each took a bedroom. Kace in the master that his parents once occupied. Adiana in the small nursery next to it.

Kace stayed in the dank, mouldy bed for a long time. Unable to get up.

Adiana busied herself with the mammoth task of repairing the house. She collected large blocks of wood and burnt a fire in the old fireplace. Desperate to capture some heat.

She climbed onto the exposed roofing and looked at it. How to fix it, she didn't know. She had no materials at hand. And if she did, she wouldn't have been able to.

She brought Kace supper each evening. A small rabbit. Or a fish from the nearby stream. Some berries. Whatever the boy could stomach.

Then Kace stopped eating and became unwell.

'You've got to eat something,' she urged, pushing a cooked fish towards him.

'This isn't appetising,' he hissed, his mood turned foul.

'It's the best I could get for you,' Adiana huffed, leaving him with the fish.

An hour or so later, Adiana sat outside and saw the fish flying out of the master bedroom window and crashing onto the overgrown grass.

'You're welcome,' she called up to the broken window and went to pick it up.

But Adiana never left him. She stayed by his side despite his sour mood and brought him food and water. He ate only when he had to, and lost a lot of weight. He looked a far cry from the well-fed boy that left the King's Town.

'I'm going to sneak into Ellon,' she said one morning after delivering him his morning berries and cup of water mixed with leaves.

'What?' Kace said, sitting up in the bed, 'you're going to what?'

'I'm going to go down into the town and steal some medication.'

'I'm fine,' Kace hissed, 'don't risk it for me.'

'I've been giving you cups of these herbal teas, but you're still hot to the touch, sweaty and as pale as if you'd never met the sun.'

'I'm just a little unwell,' Kace said, sipping the leafy water, 'I'll keep drinking this. You swear by it!'

'Exactly, and it's not working. You need something stronger.'

'I thought you didn't believe in medication?'

Adiana sighed and sat on the bed next to him, 'I don't. But I'd rather try it than have you die on me.'

'Oh, give over, I'm not going to die.'

'Kace!' She barked with a sternness in her voice that took him aback, 'this is not a two-way discussion. I shall go down into Ellon tonight, steal some medicine and be back by dawn. I'm doing it regardless. I'm just giving you the respect of telling you.'

'And if you get caught? I won't be there to rescue you like last time.' She couldn't help but think he sounded bitter in how he had said that. Like he was regretting it.

Adiana shrugged, 'Every day, I risk getting caught, shot, or eaten for your food. What's the difference?'

She left, slamming the bedroom door as she did. A silly thing for the wall was hardly there, so after her dramatics, she had to walk back into Kace's sight by passing the hole in the wall by his bedroom.

'Just be careful,' Kace said through the hole in the wall, popping a berry into his mouth.

When he knew she had gone, he painfully pulled himself from the bed. He hated her to see him like this, he really did feel quite weak.

He plodded through the empty house, his feet heavy and stupid at the end of his legs. He wandered out onto the decking in the back garden. The direct sunlight hurt him. The small walk made him oh so, weak.

He sat in one of Sander's old wooden chairs. Amazing how they still seemed solid after all these years exposed to the roughest weather. A part of his brain felt a feeling very close to pride.

The thick grass was the perfect cover for insects. Few scuttled about by the edge of the decking. Going about their little business.

It was far too big to be an insect.

Kace's eyes took a moment to adjust from the bright sun when he looked at the floor. The darkness of the thick grass shook far too violently for it to be an insect.

The creature slid from the grass with such ease that Kace feared it had been staged. The snake, with its slit black eyes, glided towards him, Kace weak with fear and illness, took too long, and the snake had death gripped itself around his leg.

The squeeze was immense.

Kace had never felt anything so strong in his entire life. The whole of the snake crushed his ankles, his feet tingled instantly with the loss of blood flow. His toes felt dead already.

The snake climbed his leg, it's fangs out and ready to bite into skin.

Kace felt overwhelmingly happy.

I'm going to see you again in a moment, Ma.

He smiled silly at the thought of being reunited with her, the sight of her open arms. As happy as he'd seen her in her wedding portrait.

But then. She was no longer there. His imagery was spoiled rotten, for her body greeted him, but her head belonged to the snake.

'I don't want to die!' He screamed suddenly. His mother with the snake head ran towards him in the vision, while in reality, the real snake was slithering up to his tor-so.

'Help!' He cried. 'Help me!'

Woof.

It was the angriest bark he'd ever heard. The sound pierced him and made him dizzy.

He fell back onto the decking with the impact of the dog. The sharp white teeth belonging to Elex punctured the snake's body.

Kace felt the blackness overcome him and passed out.

*

Sander woke crying out. Screaming. As if a demon had possessed him.

'Call the doctor!' A prison guard shouted.

Sander wailed, a vile sound to the naked ear.

'He's in trouble! Somebody help my son! Kace, he's in trouble!'

Sander continued in this vein until he tired himself out and collapsed onto the cold, stone floor.

The doctor came and diagnosed him as mentally unwell. He was to be brought to a hospital.

'We can't have a headcase like him within the walls of the King's town. People will talk.'

'My son. My son.' Is all that Sander could say.

'Send him away,' the prison warden spat with the compassion of a criminal.

And so the shaking, weak, Sander was taken out of the King's town in chains and into a horse-drawn cart bound for the only hospital in the kingdom that still routinely performed lobotomies.

A towering, horrid building just outside of Ellon. Not far from where he had come from.

Out the carriage window, between the bar spokes, Sander saw his little home town down by the sea. Then the cart took a steep climb away and up to the hospital.

My son... He whispered to the empty carriage.

*

When Adiana returned from her heist in Ellon, with a small satchel of medication, she was surprised to find Kace's bed and room empty.

'Kace?' She called to the empty house. Nothing.

'Kace?!' She walked through the kitchen and out onto the decking.

Her eyes widened at the sight. He looked so small, lay there breathing a shallow breath.

Next to him, a snake lay dead. Cold as if it had laid out all night.

It had been a cold night, and if it wasn't for the furry Elex lying beside Kace, perhaps he, too, would be dead.

'Kace!' She shook him, waking the weak dog too. Whose back left paw had a small bite mark, the size of the snake's fangs. 'Kace, please!'

Elex, understanding the task, licked the boy's face until he groggily came back around. 'Kace, talk to me.'

'Elex..' He whispered, making the dog's ears perk.

The boy's weak arm lifted, and he began to rub behind the loyal dog's ears.

'Thank you.' He whispered.

'You need to see a doctor,' Adiana said.

Kace could hardly speak. Adiana could hardly lift him. Elex was weak too.

Adiana decided she was not going to let the forest win this time.

*

The hottest topic in Ellon had gone cold.

Sander, Brithe, their son, and the mutt he ran away with.

Cold. No longer talked about as gossip. Solely now, folklore. A warning tale for children. Stay away from the dogs. They drive a person insane.

The milkmaid was the last person to see them, running free on that night from Ellon.

She was also the first to see them return.

She'd just opened the barn door for the first customer to come knocking for milk. And there. Over the hill, the three of them came.

She could only stop and stare.

The town was waking, shopkeepers opening for business, and the farmers and fishermen were off to do their thing.

Into town, they walked, the small girl carrying the small boy with the dog by her heels.

The Sheriff stepped from the town hall door.

'My word,' he said beneath his moustache.

Silence. The whole town was silent.

'Help him!' Adiana cried, dropping Kace to the cobbled floor, 'please, someone get a doctor!'

The Sheriff was unsure if he should fetch the doctor or pull his gun out and shoot the dog.

He did the former.

'Go get the doctor,' he barked at one of his men, 'it's ok, everyone, remain calm.'

The Sheriff walked forwards to them. His fingers stroked the handle of his gun affixed to his belt.

'He won't hurt you,' Adiana said. Who knows if she was talking to the dog or the sheriff?

The doctor's eyes briefly widened when he arrived at the scene, but he carried on towards them, regardless.

The town gasped under their breaths. The doctor was not about to cower in the shadows when he had a job to do.

The sheriff, too, stepped forward, perhaps not wishing to be embarrassed by the doctor's bravery.

'What happened?'

'He's been unwell for a few weeks, but last night he was attacked by a snake.'

The doctor opened his brown bag and pulled out an array of instruments.

'He would have died if it weren't for Elex,' she continued to the sheriff and, upon seeing his confusion, clarified, 'the dog.'

The sheriff glanced at Elex, clearly uncomfortable

at the idea of being so close to an alive dog.

The pink tongue hung from the dog's mouth and panted, the chocolate brown eyes avoiding the sheriff's gaze as best he could. Sneaky dog.

'He needs to get to a hospital now.' The doctor declared.

'How bad is it?' The sheriff asked.

'Bad enough to kill him without urgent help.'

The sheriff stood with the boy's life in his hands and looked around at the feared crowd. How pathetic, he thought. All this fear and unease. His town. The people he cared for, were all afraid for their lives.

The sheriff extended a hand slowly towards Elex, the crowd gasping aloud this time as he did. The sheriff's men readied their guns.

The curious dog raised his nose to the sheriff's hand and gave it a short, sharp sniff. Then gently licked it. A small lick. Just a *hello.*

The sheriff cleared his throat and pulled up his belt.

'Take the boy to the hospital.' He snapped to his men.

'Yesir,' the men chirped, going about the business.

Kace was blacked out for most of this. The jostle of movement on a stretcher woke him slightly. He looked for his mother for he was confident that he was in the afterlife. As there, standing in front of his very eyes was Elex and the sheriff himself. Side by side, like a concerned mother and father.

'Please don't hurt him,' he said desperately weak.

20.

The paradox of a hospital. A hated place, yet somewhere most go to be mended or cured. Surely a happy place? Incurable diseases are cured.

Kace was brought through to a private room on the west side. The doctor accompanied him, telling the nurses how he'd found the boy.

Modern medicine was an amazing thing, Adiana admitted as she watched her friend being injected with all sorts of liquids. She'd been lucky to remain healthy living in the forest, but here, amongst all of the little glass bottles, maybe something was to be said for a contemporary approach. Whatever saves her friend's life, she thought, that's all that truly matters.

She watched as the nurses fussed about him. Look at you, Prince Kace, she mocked in her head. She thought to remember the sight of all these lovely women around him. Oh, how you'd have loved to have been awake. The girl's retelling will have to suffice. She wanted to stand beneath a Danyan tree, and wish for him to be awake.

But he was breathing slow, shallow breaths, and that was enough for now. The gentle sound of his breath was like music to her ears. She could have gotten drunk off of the sound of his breath.

'We'll monitor him and let him rest,' the doctor had told Adiana.

'How is he?' She asked.

'He'll live. It appears to be some sort of disease in his lungs. I imagine from being out in the cold, wet elements for so long.'

Adiana pictured him lying in the mouldy, cold bed and cursed herself. If only she'd got him up and about, maybe now he wouldn't be in the hospital. She thought she'd tried her best. Perhaps her best simply wasn't enough? How can one help a person who can't even help themselves? Her mind rattled with questions, justifications and allegations.

If only she'd checked on him sooner, no matter how foul his mood was. At least she could have recognised that he was more than just beneath the weather.

A sweet-looking red-haired nurse tucked Kace into the bed, Adiana made camp next to his bed, telling them she wouldn't leave anytime soon.

'I wish I had helped him sooner,' she confided to the nurse.

'That was not your duty,' the sweet nurse smiled, 'you did the right thing bringing him here, at least.'

'Maybe for him, probably not for Elex.'

'Is that the dog's name?' The nurse asked like it was taboo to discuss. Which it was.

'Elex, Kace's dog, yes.'

The nurse was silent a moment, checked over her shoulder and took Adiana's hand gently, 'I hope they don't kill the boy's dog. Personally. I never minded them. Dogs, that is.'

'They're not vicious,' Adiana said, 'to a rabbit or a deer, *we* are vicious. But we're just surviving, really.'

The nurse contemplated this, her face conveying perhaps she was thinking about it for the first time.

'Sometimes the scariest thing is the fear itself,' Adiana said.

The nurse smiled, her freckled cheek, folding warmly. She wiped her hands on a wet towel and stepped out of the room.

'I'm not going to let them kill your dog,' Adiana told the sleeping Kace.

Perhaps he heard her, for momentarily, a little smile crept onto the side of his mouth.

The sheriff's men had carried Kace to the hospital.

'You going with the boy or the, um, dog?' The sheriff had asked Adiana.

'Where's Elex going?' Adiana asked. 'The dog.' She clarified.

'To a cell. For now.' The sheriff said.

Adiana had gone with Kace to the hospital, Elex was strong enough to defend himself, she had concluded. Kace, however, needed her. And she wasn't about to let him down again.

She sat by his side all night, only nodding off to sleep once or twice. And when she did, it was only for a few moments, before jolting awake, ready to fight any snakes that were nearby. How silly, she thought, they were safely inside the hospital now. Away from the snakes. Away from the forest.

The following day, Kace awoke, his head sore, his arms heavy and a thickness in his eyes. As if his eyelids were made of wood, he peeled them open, painfully and slowly.

The sight that greeted him was beautiful.
Friendship. Unconditional friendship.

Adiana smiled back at him, 'Good morning.'

Kace looked around the walls, the intact roof, the warm mould-free blankets, 'you've done the house up a bit.' He smirked.

Adiana laughed and asked him how he felt.

'Better than I had with a snake wrapped around me,' Kace said, sitting up. His eyes widened, suddenly.

'Where is Elex?'

'He's,' she started, 'with the sheriff.'

'What?!'

'He's ok, the sheriff gave me his word that nothing bad would happen to him.'

'For now, maybe,' Kace said, concerned, 'but what happens after I'm out of the hospital?'

'Then you can join me in protecting him,' she said, squeezing his hand, 'our arrival into Ellon was quite the scene. The sheriff won't, um, harm Elex on a whim until he gauges what the town wants him to do.'

'Surely kill him?'

Adiana looked unsure, 'One of the nurses says the town is a little divided on the matter.'

Kace waited for her to continue.

'Their whole life, the townspeople have been told that all dogs are evil, but there, in front of their very eyes, was Elex plodding loyally by our side.'

'What's going to happen now?' Kace asked after a moment of silence.

Adiana shrugged, 'Your guess is as good as mine. Who knows what a small-town in dissaray is capable of.'

It's true. The town had been bitten by something worse than a dog; a challenge to their beliefs. The thing that Ellon fears more than the dogs.

The gossip spread faster than any gossip had ever spread in Ellon. Everyone looked nervously from side to side, afraid of giving an opinion until the consensus was unanimous.

Inside a kitchen, in a small Ellon townhouse, the red-haired nurse told her parents that the boy had woken.

'And what's your opinion on it all?' They asked her.

She looked at them defiantly and said, 'Both him and his friend, the wee girl, seem lovely. They swear the dog is a good soul. Elex is its name.'

'They've named the dog? Whatever next?' Chirped the nurse's grandfather from the corner of the room.

But the following morning, when the nurses' parents chatted in the local market square, upon being asked, they shrugged and said, 'The dog seems ok. It has a name. Elex.'

The sheriff paced his office, unsure of what to do. He had written to the King's Town, but with the coronation of the new king and queen just days away, they were far too busy to respond. He didn't care to admit that he had no clue as to what to do.

At first, he had ignored his furry visitor in the furthest jail cell. His men threw in slabs of meat and buckets of water.

But curiosity got the better of him, and the sheriff

found himself outside of the cell.

'You won't bite me, will you,' he muttered pointlessly through the door.

Inside he heard the sound of paws tip-tapping on the jail cell's stone floor. They seemed almost like excited sounds. Like sounds of greeting.

He took a breath and opened the cell. Elex's tail wagged, and the dog sniffed at the frozen sheriff's feet.

'I suspect you smell my lovely wife's cooking?' He said down to the dog, then caught himself, cleared his throat and left.

The town that had ruled against the dogs was now thinking of sparing one from execution.

The word had spread fast, and despite the coronation, the King and Queen consort were pressured into speaking. Their own people mocked the little fishing town of Ellon.

'They're like young women, changing their minds every few days,' the drunk men in the King's town joked.

It seemed that the only person in the entire kingdom who didn't know the dilemma Ellon faced was Sander Di Comb himself. Who was locked in a padded cell in the very same hospital his son was walking out of.

'You're to take your medication and keep an eye on yourself, Kace,' the doctor urged.

'I'll make sure of it,' Adiana said, giving Kace a warm fuzzy feeling inside of him. To know she cared, was enough to get through any day. And there were many tough ones ahead.

'I will visit you every second day to ensure your condition remains stable. I trust you are to return home?'

'Define home,' Kace said quietly.

'He is to return to where his parents once lived, yes.'

There had been back and forth on this, a jail cell while the sheriff thought it all through, or the house Kace once lived in. The doctor had urged for the latter. Saying the boy could well become unwell again in the damp conditions of the cell.

So the sheriff had allowed the boy and his friend to return back to his home, with the stipulation that one of his men was to stand guard at the door for the foreseeable.

'House arrest?' Kace snorted.

'It's better than *real* arrest,' Adiana said, hiding her dismay at his lack of excitement on said matter. Along with the doctor, she'd fought hard to keep them out of a jail cell.

'Where is my Da?' Kace asked. 'Is he in the house?'

The doctor had looked about the room nervously at this, 'You'll have to ask the sheriff, I am not obliged to tell.'

'Is he alive?'

'Yes.'

'Is he in Ellon?'

'No.'

They were escorted out of the hospital, down the hill, through the town, along the cobbled streets and up the wooden stairs.

Their whole journey was watched like a procession. The town leant out of windows, and stood in doorways, all wanting to see the boy they once called a neighbour.

It was quite a disappointment, though. The town and their colourful imagination pictured the boy as a half-dog, half-boy.

But before them was only the scrawny boy they'd looked past many times when he lived down that cobbled street and up those wooden stairs. They tutted at the underwhelming sight.

As Kace stepped inside his old home, he couldn't help but feel a burning sensation in his eyes. Once the sheriff's officer had left his position near the entrance, Kace gave in to the overwhelming emotions and allowed himself to shed some tears.

'It's understandable to feel this way, and it's okay to let it out.' Adiana held him. Looking around at a place she'd be pleased to call home. But she couldn't say this to Kace.

'You're doing well,' she said with a rub of his shoulder. He smiled, and together, as they had done in the forbidden house, they walked from room to room in tow.

At his parents' bedroom door, Kace spent a moment breathing slowly before stepping.

'It still smells like her,' he whispered, 'is that a weird thing to say?'

'No, everyone has a smell. Not always a bad one, either.'

Kace stared at the small portrait above the large bed. It was of him, Sander and Brithe sat at their dinner table. It was funny how few personal things they had.

By the bedside table, on his father's side, sat an envelope addressed to nobody.

Kace picked it up and opened it.

Adiana felt the boy's energy turn cold. A frost had come into the room.

'I'll go heat the stove,' she said wanting to give him space.

She waited in the kitchen for him for close to half an hour. When he finally did emerge he had a blank look on his face. Not happy. Not sad.

'I, um,' she started delicately, 'I don't know how a stove works.' She confessed as the cold kettle remained so.

'What was it?' She asked plainly. To fill the silence if anything.

'A note.' Kace said weakly.

'For whom?'

'Everyone. He was saying goodbye.'

Adiana felt her stomach falling, 'He didn't go through with it, though.'

'How do we know? They could be lying,' Kace said, his eyes widening in fear.

'Why would they lie about that?'

'Well, then where is he?' Kace said in a raised voice.

'Maybe he's looking for you, Kace.' Adiana snapped back, regretting the sharpness in which it had come out.

After a moment, Kace scoffed, 'I didn't know he could write.' And then he laughed.

Adiana wasn't sure if she could join in, so she only offered a smile.

'Allow me,' he said, lighting the stove, 'tea and bed?' He offered.

She agreed with gratitude, she hadn't meant to snap at him. It was a cart full of tiredness coming down at once on her.

As she walked towards her bedroom after washing her face, she paused in the darkness of the hallway and looked up through the wooden bannisters. Kace was standing in his bedroom re-reading the letter from Sander. This had been the third time she had caught him reading it that night. After supper, he had slunk to his bedroom, then once again after his evening tea. Reading the same words repeatedly as if they would jumble into new sentences and tell him more than he already knew.

She thought it best to let him, though, so she carried on down the hallway and settled for her first sleep in a real bed. The comfort had been scary at first, but soon she felt sleep take her.

In the morning, she awoke, cushioned and content. Such a blissful sleep. Why would anyone ever care to leave this soft heavenly place? How beautiful a simple mattress and pillow were to her. She could hardly fathom ever sleeping inside a cave again.

She felt an ugly resentment for Kace, for him to have such a heavenly home and run away from it. She thought back to how she had snapped at him last night and felt guilt rush all over her.

In the crisp morning light, she stood and took some slow breaths, making a promise to herself not to get jealous and snap at her friend again.

21.

Kace couldn't fall asleep in his old bed for a few days.

He found comfort in his reading nook. The spot he'd always loved most in the house. Instead of the latest adventure novel, though, he would sit reading Sander's letter repeatedly.

The words eventually became numbing, the first gut-punching impact of them becoming fainter and fainter with each read.

He couldn't picture a world where his father was sitting writing it. The letter said he was crying as he did. Kace never saw his father cry.

The words rose up from the paper and danced inside the boy's head. In particular, the last line.

Love looks a wee bit different to us all. Mine might have looked bad, I see that now. But it was love. That's all it ever was and is.

Was it true? Had Sander loved Kace? What a rogue suggestion that he didn't, but Kace hardly ever felt loved by him.

He knew his Ma had loved him, but her sickness robbed them both. Sander's love, if you could call it that, seemed wholly unadorned.

The silent suppers, the grunts, the constant drinking and the differences. Sander and Kace were different people.

He thought about how the people of Ellon were so afraid of difference. Maybe he was just the same as them. Maybe his fear of Sander had always been based on the singular idea that he didn't understand him.

Fear is just the negative anticipation of the un-known. Hadn't he once been afraid of dogs?

Adiana stood at his bedroom door, 'Kace?'

The boy, in his nook, was startled. He fumbled with the papers, trying not to drop them.

'Sorry,' she said embarrassed 'I didn't mean to scare you.'

'No, it's ok,' he folded away the letter, and she chose not to look at it.

'The sheriff wants to speak to us. His man will es-cort us down to the town hall this morning. Our chaper-one.'

'Ok,' Kace smiled, and she left for the kitchen.

'Would you like a cup of tea?'

'Yes, please,' he called back to her. A simple domestic life.

They walked through the town towards the town hall. The morning was bright, and the sun shone just right. A single white cloud travelled across the otherwise blue sky. Like a stick on the slowest river of all time.

'This is a heavenly town,' Adiana said, looking out at the fishermen setting out for a day in the bay.

'Try living here, though,' Kace mocked.

The beauty of the town couldn't be denied. It was, at its core, a quaint little fishing village. It's just the people that could make it such an unbearable place to be.

With the rhythm of their walk, Kace fell into a reverie, thinking about how lovely the town would be if it were just him and Adiana here. He pictured living in a little house by the water, right next to his best friend in her own abode. How wonderful it would be to meet for sea swims every morning.

Like she had been reading his mind, she tugged at Kace's sleeve and pointed to the small sandy cove beside the harbour walls.

'I've never swam on a beach before,' she said excitedly.

'We'll go some time,' he promised.

At the town hall, the sheriff sat in his office waiting for them.

'Give us some privacy,' he said as one of his men brought Kace and Adiana in. 'Would either of you care for tea?'

'We've had tea, thanks.' Adiana said.

'How's Elex?' Kace asked, the question ready on his tongue for days.

'The dog is fine,' the sheriff said.

'*The dog's* name is Elex.' Kace said. 'Please call him by his name.'

The sheriff glanced over his shoulder subtly, like he was just checking that they were still alone.

'Elex is fine.' He said, then stood and poured himself a cup of herbal tea.

'I'm going to put him on trial,' the sheriff said with his back to Kace and Adiana. 'The dog.' He clarified. 'I've thought long and hard about this, and the fairest way I can think is to treat the dog like,' he paused, 'like a human.'

'I beg your pardon?' Kace said, stunned.

'The dog, um, Elex, will stand trial with a judge and jury. Its fate is in their hands.' The sheriff sat at his desk again, sipping his tea. 'A selection of jurors will be picked at random. All Ellon citizens. All parties involved will have the chance to speak, except the dog for obvious reasons, and to say their piece. And then based on that, the jury will vote whether to execute the dog or not.'

'You can't kill Elex,' Kace snapped. The sheriff raised his hand to stop him.

'This is a very sensitive case, and certain delicacy must be taken. Please, don't make this any harder than it needs to be. It will be the town of Ellon versus Elex, the dog.' The sheriff said.

Adiana believed she could pinpoint the exact moment when the sheriff had heard the sentence aloud for the first time. His eyes gave away how foolish it sounded.

'And you,' he continuted, turning to Adiana, 'as someone with no fixed abode, you are not permitted to participate in the trial in any capacity.'

'But, sir,' Kace pleaded, 'she is vital to the story of how Elex saved both of our lives multiple times. She is a witness. Without her, I'm just a lunatic alone in the forest!'

'Harsh,' Adiana whispered to Kace.

'Do you wish to become a resident of Ellon formally?' The sheriff asked her plainly.

'Does that mean I can participate in the trial?'

'All residents may participate in public trials, yes.'

'Then, yes.'

The sheriff gave a low exhale of breath, 'I can't stop you from becoming a resident. In fact, I encourage it.' He stood. 'I shall arrange for a defence lawyer to call at your house in the coming days. They can explain it all further.'

'Can I see him?'

'He'll call to your house, I just told you.'

'Not the lawyer.'

'Then who?'

'Elex.' Kace said defiantly. 'I want to see my dog.'

The dog was brimming with joy when Kace appeared at his doorway.

The sheriff watched with genuine wonder as the boy dropped to his knees and rubbed the dog's coat all over.

'Are they feeding you in here, boy?' He said into the triangular ears.

Adiana, too, stepped in and hunkered down next to the boy and the dog.

'He looks healthy,' she reassured Kace.

Behind them, the sheriff cleared his throat, 'We are feeding and watering him, yes.'

'Thank you,' Kace smiled, and perhaps for a moment, there was a flicker of one in return.

'Can I ask for one more thing?' Kace said as they were leaving the cell.

'You're pushing your luck, boy.'

'Just this one last thing. Please.' He said.

The sheriff's men were taken aback at the request.

'Watch over them as they go for a swim?' They

squawked.

'Don't question it,' the sheriff barked. 'Let them swim.'

And so, on their way back home from the town hall, the sheriff's men flanked the small sandy beach as Kace and Adiana stripped down to their underclothes and ran into the cold sea.

'How lovely,' Adiana said, floating back into the salty, waves.

'My Da and Ma got married on this beach,' Kace said.

'Is that so?'

'So they say,' Kace dipped his head into the salty cold, then emerged blowing out seawater. 'Obviously, I hadn't been born yet.'

'Obviously.'

'That portrait,' Kace said, 'From their wedding day. Was done just over there.' He pointed to a part of the beach enclosed with rocks.

'How do you know?' Adiana asked.

'I can see it from my bedroom window. I used to pray that I could magic my way back to that very spot all those years ago and warn them about my brother.'

'Maybe you should have found a Danyan tree,' Adiana said, resting her head back in the water.

'Hm, maybe,' Kace mused.

Together they floated, occasionally staring back at the beach and the surrounding fishing cottages.

Adiana admired the faraway hills that kept the forest hidden from view. Out of sight, out of mind.

The townspeople peered from their wooden shutter windows, into the sea to see the now infamous boy and the mysterious girl splashing gleefully.

Some smiled slightly, as one might when kids are seen to be having fun.

Others scowled, they were criminals in their eyes.

The town of Ellon would only become more divided before any hope of peace could be reached. This was always the nature with a town like Ellon. Those who denied such a fact lived in blissful naivety.

'A public trial over a dog,' Kace mused aloud that night.

He and Adiana sat with full bellies by the small wooden fireplace, the calming crackle of the flames sending them into a trance-like state.

'Unheard of,' he continued, 'A dog being put to trial. What a world.' He laughed a deadpan laugh. An insincere one.

'It must be a good thing?' Adiana said, unsure herself.

'If the jury is fairly picked, yes.'

'Surely it must be, there can't be a biased jury, that defeats the entire purpose.'

Kace shrugged, 'Stranger things have happened.'

'The sheriff can't risk being exposed for that sort of indecency.'

'It's not the sheriff that picks the jury,' Kace said, rubbing his eyes.

'Who does?'

*

Across town, in one of Ellon's gated communities, an off-duty judge was preparing a roast dinner.

There was a knock at the front door. Who would call at this hour, he wondered as he muttered his annoyance all the way to answering it.

'Well, hello,' the judge said, surprised to see the sheriff stood there, 'business or pleasure?' He asked, welcoming him in.

'Business,' the sheriff said, removing his hat as he entered.

'Is that so?'

'I have decided,' the sheriff said, 'to put the dog on trial.'

'I'm to trial a dog?' The judge asked like this was a completely normal request.

'Yessir,' the sheriff said, puffing his chest like he was about to justify his reasoning to an entire mob.

'Very well,' the judge said, 'would you care to join me for supper? I've cooked a lamb.'

*

Ellon did what Ellon does best. It spread the news like a tidal wave. Sweeping and foaming into every nook and cranny of the town.

Has the sheriff lost his mind? Trialling a dog!

I think it's not a bad idea, we always want more say in this town.

How has the King permitted this?

Ellon split, pro-dog trial and anti-dog trial. Taverns were filled with lively, ale fuelled debates, street corners were battlegrounds for discussion.

I don't mind the dogs, really, as long as they stay out of my town.

So many opinions. So many voices.

Too many opinions. Too many voices.

Word finally got to Sander. It was delayed, but inevitable. A progressive newspaper with a pro-dog trial article was left in the hospital common room.

Sander, heavily medicated, read it and, in a paranoid state, ran to the nurse.

'Who left this here for me to see?' He shouted. 'This is the dog that took my son.'

The doctor came and gave Sander something to sleep.

'We don't want to have to operate on your brain, do we?' The doctor said.

Sander shook his head quickly.

'You're making such good progress here, Mr Di Comb, stick with it.'

'Did somebody leave that newspaper out on purpose?' Sander asked calmly. 'Was it a test?'

The doctor smiled patronisingly, 'We're not here to test you, simply help you. In any way that we can.'

'Then get me home to my son,' Sander said through his teeth.

'Is that what you want, Mr Di Comb?'

'It's the only thing I've ever wanted, doctor.'

'I can give you that,' the doctor smiled.

'Tell me what I have to do.'

*

Not long after the news of the trial got to Sander, it also got up to the King's town. They, like always, mocked the small fishing town. Putting a dog on trial, how absurd. Only a low-class town like Ellon would be capable of such a thing, they teased.

When Flavia, in her little tavern, heard the story, she knew in her bones that the boy she had housed was the boy from Ellon.

One night, a drunk talked such foul things about him that Flavia couldn't help but snap at him.

'Maybe he's just got a bit of a backbone?'

'Don't tell me you support that rubbish,' the drunk slurred, 'a vile thing, a dog. And a boy who lies with them is awful queer to me.'

The drunk felt the full impact of a hand on the back of his head, the thump from Jaisax was mighty.

Flavia smiled at him, 'I was about to do that myself.'

'I won't have them talk badly about our wee boy.' And he returned to his glass of strong whiskey.

'Another?' Flavia offered.

'Aye, of course.'

Flavia stepped over the unconscious drunk and handed Jaisax a fresh glass.

The King had heard the news as well. The King's man stood by his side as he spoke.

'This is an embarrassment to my father's decree.' The king said.

'What do you wish to do about it, your highness?'

'Prepare my carriage, I'm to travel to Ellon tomorrow and try to talk reason into these small-town folk.'

'Very good, your highness.'

The King paced in his high castle, he looked out of the window, and very aptly, there was a dark cloud in the distance brewing a storm like a strong tea.

22.

Seemingly endless days came and went.

The winter evenings were coming, and with them came the loss of wanting to leave the house.

Kace was staying in one place for the first time in a long while. And the permanence was of comfort. Adiana whiled away the hours learning to cook using the stove, the array of different dishes she could make never ceased to amaze her. Ingredients from faraway towns she'd never heard of on the trading waters made every dish a delight.

Adiana cooked a stew with a dash of red-hot chilli pepper in it. She'd never experienced a thing like it and drank nearly the entire jug of milk while Kace rolled on the floor laughing. Wishing Elex was there to join in.

It was a nice distraction. Showing Adiana all the wonders of a modern town. But still, the boy's mind ran rampant with worry for Elex and for the trial ahead.

'An approved visitor,' the sheriff's man on duty said after knocking on Kace's door.

'Who?'

'Your counsel for the trial, I believe.'

Kace had found the men at the door surprisingly pleasant. Adiana smoothed them over by offering them cups of tea in the morning and mulled wine at night. They stood for hours at a time by the front door in all types of weather. The sight was quite the local attraction, with the townspeople taking a long way home to pass by and see the house where Kace and Adiana were kept.

'Send him in,' Kace said. But he was not a him. He was a her.

The lawyer that walked through the door was confident, immaculately groomed and had the quickest facial expressions on a person that Kace had ever seen.

'Kace?' She said. 'I am Kassandre. It's a pleasure.'

'Would you like a cup of tea?' Kace offered.

'Please,' she said, resting her leather briefcase on the kitchen table and assuming that she was invited to sit. Kace liked her already, her forwardness portrayed a confidence he lacked ahead of the trial.

'I'll do it, you talk,' Adiana said, standing from the table and going to the stove.

'So, the most famous trial in Ellon,' Kassandre started, 'the trial of a dog. How did you find yourself at the centre of this?'

'Are you asking me or yourself?' Kace joked.

Kassandre smiled slightly, 'Both.'

And so Kace told her the story of everything. He left no stone unturned, and she listened intently, only stopping to sip the occasional bit of tea.

He and Adiana had spent the days prior compiling the story down onto paper, making it razor sharp, beat by beat.

'The day you first met the dog in the forest...'

Kace leaned forward, stopping her, 'Please, I have called him Elex. That is his name. I would never speak of you as *the human,* and so I ask you to do the same in return.'

'Very well, Elex, the day you met Elex. As well

as the day he protected you from the snake. Those are the two most vivid memories I want to bring the jury into. I believe that we can spare Elex's life by conveying that we of Ellon owe him.'

'I owe him more than my life,' Kace said, his eyes ablaze.

When Kassandre had heard all she needed to, she stood suddenly, 'do you have any further questions for me?'

'I have a request,' Kace started, 'I need you to meet Elex. Before you defend him, I need you to meet him.'

Kassandre looked a little sheepish.

'It is important that you know who, not what, you are defending.' Kace urged.

'I shall arrange this for the coming week,' she said, 'that is my word.'

Kace, for the first time, felt a pang of hope. Perhaps this trial was not destined to end in tears. Perchance, Elex's life could be saved.

'If they don't kill him,' Kace pondered to Adiana that night, 'what'll happen to him?'

Adiana shrugged slightly, 'I've been wondering the same.'

'Do you think they'll let me keep him as a pet?'

Adiana snorted a laugh, 'A dog being a human's pet? Not in our lifetime.'

Kace sniffed at the absurdity, 'I suppose a man could dream.'

'You are a dreamer, Kace. But be realistic, please.'

She smiled. 'I suspect they'll release him back into the forest.'

'I guess so,' Kace mused, 'and what about you? Will you be sent out into the forest too?'

'Not if I am an official citizen of Ellon, I beg your pardon.'

Kace laughed, 'The world is a sorry place when you conform to the normalities of a town.'

'I guess,' she mused, 'I guess I'm just tired of the rough.'

*

Sander did everything necessary to please the physicians and nurses. He took his medication and went to every meeting with the doctor. Anything to not have surgery and get a chance to continue the search for his son.

'Visitor,' one of the nurses said, unlocking his room, 'Sander, this is Kassandre.'

In stepped Elex's lawyer. Just as she had in Kace's kitchen, she confidently assured herself in his little hospital room-cum-jail cell.

'I've been tasked to defend your son's dog in the trial. I have met with Kace, and I am hopeful I can spare Elex's life. In doing so, though, I will require your help.'

'What do I get out of it? Why would I protect the dog that took my son away?' Sander said.

'Because,' Kassandre smiled an earnest, yet confident smile, 'in doing so, I can get you out of here, and give you a shot at redeeming yourself in front of Kace.'

Sander stared deep into the lawyer's extensive eyes. She looked proper determined.

'I mean,' she looked around the bland room, 'what are your other options? A lobotomy here?'

*

'You will be back for the twin's birthday, won't you?' The queen consort was fussing about the King as he packed his trunk for the trip to Ellon.

'I shall,' he said, giving her a kiss, 'I must show my face in Ellon and remind them of the horrors those dogs bring.'

'And how might you do that?'

'I'll show them what they really are like.'

The queen consort didn't know what that meant exactly, but she knew her husband would not disappoint.

For he always had a plan.

In a secluded room in the King's castle, a plan was cooking. The King's head guard was busy preparing.

The King, himself, darkened the doorway.

'Your highness,' the guard said upon seeing him, 'do you care to see it?'

The King stepped into the room. The weapon, as they were calling it, was staring back at them. Chained to the wall to protect anyone who dared to enter.

The dog looked not too dissimilar to Elex.

The same shaped ears, the same inquisitive nose.

The head guard whistled a sharp whistle. The dog

stood to attention. A well-trained boy.

'No one must see us take him to Ellon,' the king said gravely.

'Of course, it is our most pressing priority, your highness.'

'Very well,' the king said with a cruel smile, 'they will thank us for doing this.'

'You don't have to justify it to me, your highness.'

'Some will die, but it is for the greater good,' the king said like he hadn't heard his guard's words of support. 'A little blood spilt to save a lot more.'

'It is, your highness.'

'The greater good.'

The dog watched them, not quite understanding what they wanted him to do. But the humans were his masters, so whatever it was, he was prepared to do it.

*

A confident Kace stepped out the front door.

'Where you off to, kid?' The sheriff's man on duty asked.

'May I just cross the road to the bakery, please? You can, of course, come with me.'

The sheriff's man was more bored than he was unsure. So, together they crossed the cobbled street and walked into the bakery.

The few customers all whipped their hands like a naked person had just walked in. A few whispers slipped from lips into ears.

Wyeth looked up, it was like he'd seen a ghost, 'Kace...'

'You remember me,' Kace joked and looked around the now deadly silent bakery. 'I'm not infectious, everyone, don't worry.'

A few chuckled nervously.

'I'm just a boy,' Kace said plainly, 'the same one that walked unnoticed around this town before. I don't bite. I'm not infected with some sort of deadly virus. I'm still just a wee boy with feelings. A whole range of them, you know, too.'

Kace smiled, 'This is me happy.'

He dropped it into a frown, 'Sad.'

He scrunched his face up and showed his teeth, 'angry. See, aren't you lot all of those things too? I'm not a monster coming over the hill. I'm just a wee boy.'

The sheriff's man gave Kace a prod, 'Get your bread and let's go, come on.'

Kace turned to Wyeth, 'Your freshest and finest loaf, me old pal.'

The baker's son took a loaf from the stove. As fresh as they get. And wrapped it in brown paper for the boy.

'Put it on my account,' Kace said with a smile and left the bakery.

Kace and Adiana sat at the wooden table and ate the fresh bread. Adiana savoured every watery bite.

'This bread melts, you know,' she exclaimed, 'and with the butter and jam. Wow.' She marvelled at it.

Kace smiled, 'Life is full of these simple wee pleasures.'

'What's your dream meal?' She asked.

'Mmm,' Kace mused, 'my Ma used to make a pickled carrot soup that I'd always have when sick, I guess it's got to be that. It cured me every single time.'

'And what's your dream for the future?' She asked unprompted.

'I guess it'd be nice to live for a bit. Or just some pickled carrot soup.'

'More bread?' She offered, reaching for the wooden chopping board.

23.

Throughout the week, Kassandre visited the house frequently, with her piles of paperwork increasing in height and her questions becoming more specific.

'When you were alone in the forest, was there ever the opportunity for Elex to kill and eat you?'

'Of course,' Kace said, 'he could have torn my arms and legs off easily if he had wanted to. But he wouldn't ever do that.'

'Ok, that's going to help us a lot, you see,' she wrote furiously as they spoke, her handwriting illegible but detailed.

'I have sought permission from the sheriff,' Kassandre started as she packed up her case of notes, 'to visit him. Elex that is.'

'May I come?' Kace said, his eyes widening.

'I'm heading there now,' she said, not answering his question in the slightest.

'And can I come? I want to see him.'

It took one of the sheriff's men to run for permission, but Kace was allowed to go with Kassandre.

'Adiana, come with us!' Kace jumped around the house excitedly. He'd been slightly put out by her all day. She had seemed slightly not herself.

'No, you go. I'll prepare supper.'

Kace wouldn't let that dampen his spirits. Together with the sheriff's men in convoy, he and Kassandre went to the town hall and found the sheriff.

'How has he been?' Kace asked before Kassandre could remove her long coat.

'Easy, Kace. He's been well, I think. I don't know much about dogs, do I?'

Kace gave him space to continue.

'It is a little odd,' the sheriff started, 'he doesn't appear to be eating as much as when he first came in.'

'Well, yes, would ye be hungry if ye were locked up all day and all night?' Kace exclaimed.

'I suppose not.'

'He's a wild animal,' Kace explained dumbly, 'he's used to hunting his food, running around and doing whatever to survive. He's not built for a jail cell.'

'Can we see him?' Kassandre interjected, impatiently, wanting to get on with her day.

The sight of Elex took Kace off guard. He almost turned to the sheriff and asked where the *real* Elex was.

Barely able to stand up was a thin, shell of a dog. His eyes drooped low, his body looked shaky.

'Elex!' Kace cried, running into the cell and embracing him, 'how can you say he's *been well?* Look at him!'

Kassandre noted how the sad droopy dog became considerably more animated when the boy entered the jail cell.

'I told ye, he's not been eating his food.' The sheriff defended.

'It's quite inhumane in here,' Kassandre said,

234

looking at the puddles of pee and piles of his darkening, stinky mess.

'He's not a human, is he?' The sheriff said.

'He has a pronoun, I'd suggest that's worthy of getting his mess cleared up.' Kassandre snapped back.

The sheriff huffed, 'I have far too much to be getting on with than cleaning up after a dog!'

'Then let me look after him,' Kace said.

'Absolutely not!'

'Well, then you shan't have a dog to put on trial in a week's time.' Kace said, his voice cracking slightly. The sheriff's eyes gave away the smallest hint of panic at that.

'Why do you think that?'

'Look at him,' Kace said desperately, 'he'll die if he stays in here.'

Kassandre stepped in front of the sheriff, 'the entire land is watching Ellon, right about now. What's going to happen to the dog? They're all wondering. Do you think that his early death in the jail cell will reflect well on the type of place you run?'

The sheriff wiped his forehead with the sleeve of his shirt, which was damp with sweat, a sticky sweat, no less.

'I'll call a vet,' the sheriff announced, 'and get their opinion.' He left, recklessly leaving Kace alone with Elex. He looked up at the lawyer.

'You can pet him,' Kace said gently.

Kassandre, like she'd been a little curious, stepped forward into the cell. Her long fingers reached out and stroked the weak dog's head. She ran her fingers along his ears.

'They're softer than I expected them to be,' she mused.

'You should see him when he's healthy,' Kace said proudly.

Kassandre eyed them both, sure of anything, that the boy and the dog had a bond. They trusted each other. And she couldn't help but feel moved by it.

A vet turned up, finally. A nervous one, but a vet nonetheless.

'I know horses and I know cows,' he said to the sheriff, "I can take a look, but I not know dogs.'

As soon as the vet stepped into the cell, he briefly glanced at Elex and turned back to the sheriff, 'Yes, of course, he's unwell. Look at him. You don't need to be a vet to know that.'

The sheriff looked more panicked, suddenly.

Kassandre stepped forward to him.

'Let the boy care for him,' she urged.

'Is there any medication we can give him?' Kace asked.

'Nutrients is most likely the best option. He needs proper food and vitamins. I can inject some of the latter in, but he needs, quite frankly, to be out of here.' The vet gestured to nothing in particular.

'Fine,' the sheriff said in a small voice, 'you can take him back to your house. But I will have two armed men at the door at all times. Day and night. If he tries to escape or makes any trouble, he will be shot dead, understood?'

'He won't cause any harm.' Kace said.

'Thank you,' Kassandre said, knowing this could only be good for the dog.

'Let me arrange the details,' the sheriff said, stepping away from the cell, his head spinning.

Alone now, the vet turned to Kace, 'What's his name?'

'Elex,' Kace said with a smile.

And the vet lowered his hand for the dog to sniff at. 'Do you smell my horses?' The vet asked the dog in a voice Kassandre found odd. An almost childlike voice. She studied it all, Kassandre. And she realised that perhaps man and dog could establish a bond of companionship. And maybe it might just look quite sweet.

The fire of gossip in Ellon was just embers when a brand-new fresh log was thrown on; the sheriff and two of his men were seen escorting the boy and the dog through the town and up the cobbled street to his home.

'This is insanity!' One of the braver townspeople shouted out. 'Ye can't be seriously letting that dog walk amongst us?'

The sheriff shouted loudly to the gathered crowd, 'It is for the best. The dog will be watched at all times by two armed men. I can assure ye that safety is my number one concern.'

Some gruntled townspeople shouted about impeaching the sheriff immediately, some told those people to shut up, and others remained quiet. Who knew what they were thinking?

They all gawked at the dog, who looked considerably less scary than the fables they'd heard behind closed tavern doors. The dog plodded along slowly, with heavy clumpy paws.

Adiana leant out of the window, the sight of Kace, Elex, and their entourage walking towards the house brought a cheery smile to her face.

Kace looked up at her, and although she couldn't hear him, she was sure that he had mouthed; *I'm bringing him home.*

That night, Kace and Adiana lay by the crackling fire. Elex, too, rested his head on the soft blanket they'd given him.

'He looks happy,' Kace said.

'He does.'

Kace turned to Adiana, oh how clean she looked now that she had access to constant warm water. 'Are you ok?'

She looked at the floor, 'today would have been my mother's birthday.'

Kace followed her eyes down, then took his hand and gave hers a squeeze.

A solitary salty tear streamed down Adiana's cheek, 'It's silly. Sorry, I know I'm being awful silly.'

'You're not being silly.' Kace squeezed her hand harder, grounding her again.

He allowed his friend to cry for an extended period of time. It might well have been the first time she had cried for her mother after her death, or potential death even. He couldn't stop his mind from being self-centred and drifting towards thoughts of his own mother. He felt fortunate to have those memories of her, no matter how insignificant they may seem in comparison to her death. At least they were something and that was the only thing he could focus on. Anything else was far too scary.

As Kace held his friend, Elex stood too, with tired and weak bones, and limped towards the crying girl. He rested his head on her lap and as the tears cascaded he licked at them helpfully.

'Thank you,' Adiana whispered to both the boy and the dog, 'how lucky you were to have this once. If only for a moment.'

Kace swallowed the lump sat in his throat, how foolish he felt.

*

The King and his entourage of most trusted guards stood on the outskirts of Ellon. Utterly undetected and hidden from view.

'On your command, your Highness.'

The King gave a curt nod. It was only fitting that this was to be his first act as King since his father had died. The man had decreed against the dogs, and the King would protect that in honour of his late father.

The King climbed up into his carriage, here was as

good a place as any.

A guard in thick armour climbed out of a separate carriage and went to the steel cage atop the following trailer. Inside the cage was the dog.

'Go cause havoc in Ellon,' the King uttered out of the window as the four paws jumped from the cage and started to sniff the ground.

The dog walked off on its own accord down the hill toward Ellon.

24.

The night before Elex's trial, Kace had trouble sleeping. He tossed, and he turned uncomfortable through the dark night.

Next door, he heard the choir of Adiana's bedsprings too.

The only one of the three able to sleep soundly was Elex himself. Who lay by Kace's feet at the end of his bed, blissfully unaware of what was ahead.

Kace found comfort in the gentle sound of his breathing, which allowed him to enjoy a few hours of rest. If not sleep, at least he was resting.

The night before, they'd stayed up late with Kassandre, sitting by the fireplace preparing an answer for every question they might get.

When their lawyer had left, shortly before midnight, Adiana and Kace had given Elex a bath. There were few things that they could control about this trial, but how Elex appeared was one of them. Adiana and Kace meticulously groomed their furry canine, taking extra care to clean the nooks and crannies that the dog's tongue couldn't reach and the river couldn't thoroughly wash. Surprisingly, they noticed that the dog's coat was much lighter than their initial perception, revealing a beautiful golden hue after scrubbing him silly with soap.

Adiana knocked on the door to Kace's bedroom, 'Good morning,' she said gently through the door, knowing he'd be awake.

Elex jumped from the bed to greet Adiana, his tail smacking the doorframe with its happiness.

She gave him a good morning pet and looked at Kace, who sat dressed now on the edge of his bed.

'Are you ready?' She asked rhetorically.

They didn't eat much before setting off for the courthouse. On either side, they were flanked by armed men, with large helmets.

It's like one could smell or hear the atmosphere in the town. It was potent. It buzzed. The townspeople talked about this day as if it were the Crossball world cup final.

They lined the streets as the procession made their way to the courthouse.

Twelve jurors had been assembled. All citizens of Ellon. All claiming not to know anything about the case. But there wasn't a person in Ellon that didn't know. The judge had stopped asking if anyone knew anything about it, and picked twelve of the best at random.

The courthouse was surrounded by people. Some even had picnics, and tents to camp out in.

'People love an occasion,' Kace whispered to Adiana as they were ushered through the gawking crowd and into the courtroom.

Some people trickled away, only appearing so as to get a glimpse of the dog in question. Who seemed to be enjoying all the attention on him.

Kassandre marched down the hall towards them, 'Gameday.' She said with a smile.

Unsurprisingly, the courtroom was full. At the top were two tables, the defence and the prosecutor, overseen by the high judge's chair, the row of benches for the jurors and in the corner, a cage with hay and a bowl of water in it.

'Hay?' Kace turned to Kassandre, 'He's not a horse.'

'How were they to know what dogs like?' Kassandre replied.

'A blanket, maybe?' Kace said, 'he's not some sort of creature from another planet.'

Kassandre asked the sheriff, 'Can we get Elex a blanket?'

'Blanket..' the sheriff muttered, walking away to retrieve one.

The first day was quite the let-down, really. Kace had been fired up for war, but instead, the judge just went about addressing the jury as well as and setting out ground rules for all those present.

'Speak when spoken to,' he repeatedly reiterated to the courtroom, 'no interjections will be tolerated. This will not become a circus of monkeys.'

He gave the room a sharp dismissive wave.

'We'll start tomorrow morning at dawn.'

Outside the courthouse, the crowd seemed to be in a dull mood too. They must have expected a metaphorical explosion to witness. Alas, it was only a day of formalities and paperwork.

The following day brought more excitement.

The prosecutor was a ratty-looking man who was very tall and uncoordinated. He had the longest nose Kace had ever seen on something that wasn't a horse. He was part human, part rat, part horse.

'Your honour, we cannot let this dog live. Over the course of this week, I shall give plenty of reasons why but ultimately, we must remember it is against the King's law not to execute a captured dog. And if we are to take liberty in that law, what might be next? Murder on the street? Robbery? We have a duty as a town to uphold the law. Look at the vile creature,' the prosecutor pointed towards the cage where Elex was lying, sleeping soundly, with the occasional silly snore. Kace tried to stifle his laugh at the thought of how this prosecutor was portraying Elex, versus how the dog *really* was.

Kassandre stood next to speak, and the entire room marvelled at the way in which she held the courtroom's attention. A real professional here, thought Kace.

'If a man was to save a young boy's life, he'd be commended and given a medal by the sheriff himself. Here, we are not asking for that, we are simply asking for the life of this furry animal to be saved. We don't expect anyone to condone the dogs, or even become friends themselves with one. We are not here to preach a radical pro-dog manifesto to ye. We simply want to thank the dog for his service to man. If we don't and we kill him,' she paused to shake her head gravely, 'then I fear we are no better than any wild animals. Be better, Ellon.'

The day carried on in this vein, the judge asked questions to both Kassandre and the ratty prosecutor. The jury listened intently with the foreman writing copious notes as they spoke.

Every so often, Elex would stir, and the courtroom would fall silent. Some hoped for drama, the prosecutor, in particular, probably wished Elex would suddenly go feral and show everyone his teeth. But he didn't. He would only stand, and circle the spot a couple of times before lying back down with a great sigh.

We'll be home soon, Kace tried to shout with his eyes.
I know, the chocolate drops said back.

On the third day of the trial, the momentum was beginning to lull. Back and forth, the same things were being said, *kill the creature,* vs *save the dog.*

Kassandre and the rat went back and forth, telling anecdotes and providing insights from animal and medical professionals.

'Can humans and dogs form a friendship?' The prosecutor asked.

'Not that I'm aware of,' replied the wild animal expert that they'd put on the stand.

Kassandre stood, 'is there any evidence of this?'

The expert said, 'It is only my opinion.'

Kassandre, 'opinion. Take note of that, please, jury.'

The judge raised his hairy hand, 'No interruptions, please, defence. You'll have your chance to ask questions at the end.'

After lunch, Kassandre stood loudly and proudly at the top of the room.

'Who do you wish to call now?' The judge asked. The room felt an odd sticky, Kace thought.

It was the afternoon hump when one feels heavy with lethargy.

'I call Sander Di Comb to the stand, sir.'

Kace was caught off guard when his lawyer mentioned his father's name, causing him to take a long while to process the information.

When he finally turned, Sander was halfway up the aisle to the stand. Those in the gallery were muttering. The prosecutor's tall frame stiffened.

'It's my Da,' Kace whispered to Adiana who had felt the sudden energy of the room change. It was as if a lightning bolt of energy had crashed into the room.

'Mr Di Comb was not on the approved list of witnesses,' the prosecutor said standing suddenly.

'Mr Di Comb is the father of Kace Di Comb,' Kassandre snapped back, 'he is a valuable witness.'

'Then why was he not on your list?'

The judge leant forward, 'prosecution makes a valid point, why is he being brought in now.'

Kassandre walked to the judge with a brown stained roll of paper, 'he has been in hospital seeking medical attention. Only this morning did his doctor approve him to testify.'

The judge took the letter and read it quickly, the type of quick read professionals do, 'very well,' he said, 'Mr Di Comb, you may step up to the stand.'

His father had grown a long straggly beard, his eyes looked tired and what was once a strong workman's frame seemed to droop like a dying flower.

Father and son locked eyes, no words being said, yet all the words in the world.

'Mr Di Comb,' Kassandre started, 'I'm going to ask you three questions and then the prosecutor will stand up and most likely ask a load of nuanced questions in a similar vein, but,' and she spun to the jury for this, 'I want you to remember, members of the jury, the answer to these three questions.'

Sander nodded, cleared his throat and leant forward.

'Mr Di Comb, did a dog attack and kill your first-born baby boy all those years ago?'

'Yes.'

'Mr Di Comb, did your second-born son run away from home into the forest with a dog?'

'Yes.'

'Mr Di Comb, do you think Elex should be sentenced to death?'

'No.'

The courtroom erupted into a frenzy of voices.

'Silence!' The judge shouted, 'Silence, please!'

'You see,' started Kassandre, 'these three questions have all been answered truthfully here in the eyes of the law. These answers are given on the basis of unconditional love. The love that one has for another living thing'.
'Unconditional love. It makes people do the most barbaric of things, isn't that right, Mr Di Comb?'

Sander leant forward again, 'Yes. I am not proud of some of the things I've done to keep my son safe.'

'Such as?'

'Chasing him through the forest, hiring somebody to track him…' Sander trailed off.

'Would you wrestle a snake if it were attacking him?'

'Of course, I would.'

Kassandre turned to Elex and softly said, 'So, do you think that this dog is capable of unconditional love?'

'I, um, believe there may be proof of that, aye.'

Sander said hardly looking at the dog.

'When you heard that Elex here had saved your son's life, did you change your answer to the last of my three questions?'

'I did,' Sander whispered.

'What was your answer before?'

'That the dog should be killed.'

'But now?'

Sander looked deep into Kace's eyes, 'Now I don't. I may never understand their *friendship* but I can learn to accept it.'

'Do you hold resentment against dogs after your firstborn was killed by one?'

Sander felt his eyes stinging, 'I did. But not anymore.'

'And what changed your mind, Mr Di Comb?'

'Because,' he cleared his throat, 'don't we all deserve a second chance?'

Kassandre bathed in the silence of the courtroom, then smiled a genuine smile at Sander as his eyes silently cascaded tears, 'that is all,' she said with a curt nod.

'Anything from the prosecution?' The judge said.

The tall man tapped his pencil against the paper on his desk, the only sound in the courtroom, 'Your honour, we do not have any questions at this time.'

Kace watched as his father stood and walked out of the courtroom. The now weak-looking carpenter avoided all possible eye contact with his son. Perhaps, he thought the tears would be a sign of weakness and he didn't wish Kace to see. Oh, how weak you look, anyway, Kace thought, coming back down into the room.

He realised that Adiana had taken hold of his hand and was squeezing it tight. Little reassuring squeezes that only they knew.

The judge turned to Kassandre, 'No more surprise witnesses will be permitted, understood?'

'Yes, your honour,' she chirped, sitting back at her desk.

From the open door in which Sander had exited, a blue and black butterfly floated into the courtroom. A few of the gallery chuckled at the absurd little insect as it cut through the stark, stoic courtroom. Its bright and vibrant colours grabbed everyone's eye.

It fluttered towards the cage where Elex was lying watching it. The wings brushed against the steel bars as it slipped into the dog's pen.

Sitting up erect, Elex gave the butterfly a perfect place to land. His wet nose.

The butterfly landed and rested its wings on Elex's coal-black nose.

The entire courtroom watched on, and a few of the more brave people giggled.

Then in a great huff, Elex found his nose friend ticklish and sneezed loudly, sending the butterfly up and out of the cage.

Kace and Adiana laughed first, followed by nearly everyone in the courtroom.

Even the judge himself rumbled a deep laugh from his large belly. And while it could have been a trick of the light, but Adiana swore that she even saw the prosecutor stifle a comic grin.

If fear is destined to divide, then laughter is the only antidote in which to unite.

25.

The trial continued on, but it was like it had lost its sting. The fear that the courtroom once had towards Elex had numbed. The occasional person even walked up to the cage and glanced in at the confused dog. Man will always cage the exotic and stare at it until it becomes ordinary. Slow creatures, slowly understanding the world around them.

Kace felt an elated feeling for the first time in a long while. In fact, it was more than that. Something more powerful; hope.

The judge leant forward in his seat, 'Defence, you may call your next witness to the stand.'

Kace stood and walked towards the seat his father had sat in the day previous. It couldn't have been, but he swore he smelt the man's oaky must lingering in the booth. The smell was synonymous with his childhood.
He'd recognise it anywhere.

Kassandre smiled and nodded to signal that she was about to begin.

'Kace Di Comb, we heard from your father yesterday. Quite an emotional day for us all. How was it for you?'

'Bittersweet,' Kace said honestly, 'he is my Da, after all. That's a type of love that can't ever be explained. For better or worse.' Kace added as an afterthought.

'I hope you don't find this condescending, Kace, but you're very emotionally intelligent for your years.'

'Too much so, maybe,' Kace said to a few chuckles.

'How would you describe Elex?'

Kace looked to the ceiling as if the answer was there, then back sternly at his audience, 'Elex is a living being who feels emotion, empathy and loss. Just like us.'

'And why don't you believe he should be sentenced to death.'

'For what crime?' Kace pierced through the room. 'The crime of being different?' Kace asked rhetorically.

'His existence,' Kace continued, 'is in our hands, we have a duty of power and protection over those that don't. What moral compass are we following if we kill an innocent life just because we fear what it could do? That is not a world I care to be a part of.'

Kassandre gave a wry smile and looked at her notes.

The prosecutor walked up to Kace and he saw how faded the man looked. His eyes drooped low, sags of bags beneath them. A tired old man.

'Kace,' he started, 'what did you have for supper last night?'

Confused, Kace leant back in his seat, with the eyes of the courtroom on him, 'I had a pie, sir.'

'A pie,' the prosecutor repeated loudly, 'what was in your pie?'

'Potato, steak and vegetables.'

'Steak,' the prosecutor repeated, 'steak from a cow?'

'Yes, steak from a cow.'

'Do you value a cow's life?' The prosecutor asked.

'I,' Kace looked around the room, 'I do, of course.'

'Yet, you have no problem eating a slaughtered cow? But you, and I quote, wouldn't care to be a part of a world where the moral compass kills innocent life.'

The prosecutor gave an ugly smile.

'A dog kills and eats humans, your very own big brother, for example, yet a cow only eats grass. But you do not condone the execution of the dog, while you eat an innocent cow?' The tall man hunched forward, pacing the floor dramatically. 'Doesn't make much sense to me, Kace.'

Kassandre's face conveyed a worried expression. For the first time, it looked like there was something she hadn't considered.

'Have you ever seen a cow licking its calf clean in the field?'

'Probably,' Kace replied.

'So, cows can have love and empathy too? What do you propose next, we stop killing cows. And lambs? And chickens?'

Kassandre stood, 'Your honour, this questioning is neither here nor there and doesn't relate to Elex directly.'

'Oh, but it does,' the prosecutor snapped back, 'if the boy's point is that of moral righteousness, then perhaps he should be morally right throughout.'

When Kace couldn't find the words to answer, and the silence went on for too long, the prosecutor whipped out, 'No further questions for now.'

Kace looked at the peaceful Elex, who was becoming used to this weird daily charade of being paraded in the cage. As quick as he'd experienced the hope, he felt an overwhelming sense of dread. Nuance doesn't have a home in this small town, and to underestimate its simplicity is to ask for trouble.

I wouldn't want to be on that jury, the town whispered in gossip.

Again, the trial had reheated to a toasty finale. What had once become cold, was the talk of the town again. But it was less about Kace, or even Elex or the trial itself.

It's simple!

Animals are for killing and eating.

But we don't eat horses? Far more meat on a small horse than on a big dog.

They work for us, though.

The town had always prided itself on black-and-white morals, but now, there was shade. And they didn't find that all too comfortable. It made their brains have to think too hard. The effort was far too much.

If we spare the dog, it's unfair to all the cows we kill!

So dogs are better?

Not what I'm saying!

Again, so many opinions and so much noise.

Kace and Adiana lay by the fireplace in their home. Kace stroked Elex's sleeping head.

'We could run,' he said.

'Haven't we run enough?'

'More than enough,' Kace said, scolding himself at

the impulse to run. He was here and fighting.

'As someone who has been in the wild their whole life,' Kace said, 'what are your thoughts?'

'Eat or be eaten,' Adiana said matter of factly.

'And if you lived here?'

Adiana looked more unsure now, 'I guess I can't speculate what I'd do if I had access to all of that lovely meat.'

She prodded the stew on the table before her, and Elex raised his head to beg.

'It's too complicated, you know.' She said giving Elex a chunk of lamb. 'They were always going to throw a big moral conundrum into the centre of this, to distract the jury. That's what all the crime writers do.'

Kace pondered this, 'I suppose.' Then his face went puzzled a moment. 'How can you read?'

'Hm?' Said Adiana, taking her own chunk of lamb.

'You were raised in the forest? With your Ma?'

Kace watched how she closed her body as if she was defending herself from a snake attack.

'You,' he said slowly, 'you weren't raised in the forest, were you?'

The words were like little jabbing needles. 'Kace…' She said gently.

'You lied to me,' he said.

'Please don't be mad at me, I..'

'I'm not mad,' Kace stammered, 'I'm just confused why…'

But Kace could not finish his sentence as the horn from outside made Elex startle awake and bark wildly.

'Calm down, boy!'

'What is it?'

Kace and Adiana ran to the front door, locking the barking Elex in the kitchen.

They opened the door to a commotion, people gathered in nighties by their front door, too.

'What is it?' Kace asked the man on duty at their door.

'The King.' He said sombrely.

'Pardon?'

'The King has ridden into Ellon,' the sheriff's man said.

Sure enough, in the distance, they could see the swarm of armed King's guards sweeping behind the golden carriage.

The crowd muttered nervous gossip and followed the procession towards the king's Ellon residence. A house that has not been used by the monarch's family since the decree against the dogs all those years ago.

'It's hardly a coincidence,' Kace said, later that evening, 'that the king would arrive in Ellon unannounced randomly in the middle of the trial.'

'What are you saying? That he's here for the trial?'

'I think he might well be,' Kace said gravely.

'They can't allow the king to be a part of the trial, surely?'

But they did.

The following morning, the king himself was brought to the courthouse, where the prosecutor, more giddy than ever, called him to the stand.

'Your honour,' Kassandre pleaded, 'it is totally unfair to expect a fair trial where the king is a witness!'

'Is the defence's argument not that humans and dogs should be treated equally? Then why would the king not be allowed to be called up to the stand like any other man, woman or child?'

'It is absurd!' Kassandre cried.

'Do you want equality?'

The judge stopped them, 'Please, this is most bizarre, but I will have to permit His royal highness to be a witness. To keep a person off of the stand is not what this court stands for.'

And so, the courtroom stood when the king entered and was escorted to the witness stand. The court sheriff stood before the king and fell into his usual speech.

'Do you swear on the, um, king's life to tell the whole truth and nothing but the truth?'

'I swear on the king's life,' the king replied to a couple of subtle giggles and Kassandre rolling her eyes.

'Your Highness,' the prosecutor said, standing before him 'may I be so forward as to ask what your late father was most proud of during his reign as king?'

'It was always the fact that his decree against the dogs had saved many lives of his people.'

'Can you remember those days before the law came into place?'

'I was young, but of course, I remember the tension in the air of my father's people. I remember the stories he'd tell of how frightened everyone was.'

'And when the decree came in?'

'Well, wasn't it just the most elated feeling for all? People could relax and no longer fear that wild dogs would roam the street and snatch their young.' The king said this last bit looking directly at Kace. 'He spoke fondly of that day, my father did, how the sun had shone aptly all day, and the skies were beautifully blue. Do all of you Ellon folk remember that?'

The courtroom seemed to slip into the ideal, happy memory.

'They say everyone remembers where they were when the dogs were banned?' The King continued, his powerful ability to hold an audience on show, 'I ask the entire court here today where they were? Picture that moment. How joyous an occasion it was. Simply splendid. Don't spoil that memory.'

The questioning continued in this vein until the prosecutor asked him outright, 'Do you, your Highness, think that this dog should be sentenced to death?'

Kassandre stood quickly, 'objection, his royal highness can't be asked to answer with his *opinion* in a public trial. That is too far.'

The King raised his ring-covered finger and answered for the judge, 'It is correct, as the head of the state, it would be inappropriate for me to give a personal opinion on a matter as this, however,' he looked at Elex in the cage, 'my father started this war against the dogs for a reason. He was not a weak man, and I hope the people of Ellon are not weak either. That is all I will say.'

The prosecutor turned to Kace and gave him a sly wink as he sat.

Kassandre, who looked as pale as a white wall, stood and cleared her throat, 'Your Highness.' She said and looked around the quiet courtroom, all waiting with bated breath to see if she would cross-question the king, 'Your Highness...' She trailed off and then turned to the judge. 'I have no questions at this time, your honour.' And sat. Kace leaned forward and rubbed his eyes slowly.

He felt Adiana's reassuring hand on the small of his back.

In the silence, the judge spoke loud and clear, 'Jurors, you will be escorted to a room to deliberate. When you decide, the foreman will stand before this very court and declare whether the dog is innocent or guilty. If found guilty, the dog will be sent for execution.'

The judge stood and dismissed the jurors. Each of them shuffled out the door next to Elex's cage. They all took one last look into the cage. Elex wagged his tail at the attention.

By the fireside, Kace and Adiana sat numbly stroking Elex's head. The jurors were still in deliberation. It had been six hours, and the night was closing in fast.

'I don't think we're going to hear today,' Adiana said.

Kace sluggishly said, 'No, I should expect not.' And after a moment of silence had elapsed, he spoke again, 'Where are you from?'

Adiana had been waiting for him to pick up the conversation.

'I ran away from my home,' she said, 'A while ago. So, long ago.'

'Why?'

'Why did you?'

'I was chased out.'

'Same,' she said softly. 'My mother was not very good to me. She may as well have raised me in the forest, for we moved so frequently.'

'Where is she now?'

Adiana shrugged, 'I haven't seen her in years. I do suspect she might well be dead. Not by the forest, but by something worse, I suppose.'

Kace took his friend's hands and squeezed them, 'I promise. When all this is over, you, me and Elex will go out to find her. If my da can say what he said in court, yours is out there wanting you too.'

'I don't know,' Adiana said, closing her body, 'life doesn't come with fairytale endings, Kace.'

'Do you really believe that?'

'What evidence do I have to prove the opposite? Life is just tough. It's gritty and full of hard work. It's survival of the fittest, we all go through bad times, and it can just suck.'

'But the people make it beautiful. Like single green shoots in a bed of dying flowers. That's all life is good for. Connection, be it, humans or animals.'

'Oh, Kace, you are a dreamer.'

Morning came with a loud, full knock at the front door. The sheriff's man said they were to go to the court-room immediately. Word spread quickly that the jury had come to deliberation, and despite the early hour, everyone in the town was shuffling towards the courthouse steps.

Kace and Adiana paraded the dog, flanked by the sheriff's men. Passing the king's residence, Kace glanced up and saw the man standing regally on his balcony, looking down at them. The king smiled a dirty one.

The courtroom was full, of course, and even Sander had been allowed to come to watch.

Kace smiled at him helplessly, he wished for the chance to talk to him.

All rise, the judge entered and sat on his towering chair.

'Please bring the jury in,' he told the court sheriff.

They shuffled in like little disobedient schoolchildren.

'Foreman, have you reached your decision on whether the dog is innocent or guilty?' The judge asked.

The foreman, who looked unremarkable in all counts, stood and cleared his throat.

'We have, your honour.'

Elex, sitting in his cage, seemed to perk up at the sound of a new voice. His tail dropped a loud wag. Just the one, *Thump.*

'And what is your decision?' The judge asked.

'Your honour, we have unanimously found the dog to be guilty.'

Kassandre dropped her head and began to pack away her papers.

The prosecutor celebrated with the quick shake of

a balled fist.

Kace tried all he could not to, but he stood and cried out, 'No!'

Adiana let tears roll down her cheeks.

Sander stood too, his face red, 'Are ye all mental?' He shouted, causing the sheriff's men to grab him.

'Well,' the judge stated, 'the dog will be sentenced to death at midnight tonight.'

He snapped his gavel down loudly, and the courtroom erupted, some cried, and some cheered. The stoic jury members were taken from the room.

Kace and Adiana hugged tightly, crying. Unable to bring themselves to look at Elex.

Sander's violence rose, and he was taken from the courtroom in handcuffs, shouting for his son.

Elex, meanwhile, lay watching these humans being weird, what were they all doing, he wondered, but quickly lost interest as behind his ear, he had an itch that needed attention.

It was a good scratch.

26.

A lush green meadow with streaks of golden sun coming from the bodies of the trees. A sight so beautiful as the dog bounds towards them. Ears bouncing up and down. His tail wags behind him as he runs.

Come here, Elex!

The black nose is like a travelling dot with two brown chocolate buttons above it.

This is neither a dream nor an imagination.

It's a memory.

From deep within the forest, the boy had seen the dog run.

Now, though, he watched him slipping away in the cage.

'Elex!' He cried, trying to push his way through the line of sheriff's men, behind him, Adiana pleaded with Kassandre.

'Can't we appeal immediately? Do something! Do anything!'

Kace managed to push his way through, slipping like the small child he was beneath their arms, and he ran to the cage.

Elex jumped up at the sudden rush from the boy. Hello master, his eyes said.

'Please, you can't kill him. I will do anything. I will rot in jail myself!'

As painful as it was for the onlookers, they couldn't take their eyes off of the screaming boy and his friend.

The door was shut with the caged dog on the other side.

'I beg you all to leave this courtroom,' the sheriff urged as his men began to shepherd the crowd towards the exit.

Kace dropped to the floor and refused to leave. Finally, alone again, he and Adiana looked at each other.

'I'm not letting them kill him,' he said.

'I'm not letting you let them kill him,' she said.

Outside the courthouse, word had spread through the gathered crowd. Those lucky enough to be in the court-room came out and recounted how the boy had cried and how angry his father was.

I never trusted that family, an odd bunch.

If ye ask me, probably for the best. Where does it go next if we spare a dog?

Ah, I feel quite bad for the dog. He seems harmless.

He's a dog! They kill!

Exactly. I think it's best if we kill it.

Kace was walking alone now with the sheriff, 'I've written a letter to your father's doctor,' he said, 'suggesting that he should be released from the hospital.'

Kace nodded numbly.

'I hope that acts as a silver lining,' he continued after a quick glance over his shoulder, 'Eh, for what it's worth, I grew quite fond of Elex when he was locked up.'

Weirdly, thought Kace, that did actually help. It wouldn't save his dog, but it felt wholesome to know that he wasn't alone and mad for loving his four-legged friend. If the sheriff could grow fond of him, then maybe, just maybe, in the future, dogs could be loved.

'Sometimes I'd throw my baton across his cell, and he'd trot to get it and drop it at my feet.' The sheriff said in a sweet voice. Before taking a sharp breath in and patting Kace on the shoulder. 'You'll be fine, kid.'

'Can we say goodbye to him?' Kace asked.

'I'll arrange that for this evening,' the sheriff said.

'How is it going to happen?'

'My men will shoot him in the head. It'll be pain-less and quick.'

Kace nodded, and the sheriff thought it best to leave him. The boy's feet kept carrying on and to the portraits of those killed by capital punishment.

It was a vile wall, Kace thought, looking at all the poorly sketched criminal faces. He wondered if they would sketch Elex's furry face and add it to their collection. Or were they not even going to give him that?

She looked so small at the end of the line of por-traits. Little confused, Adiana, stood staring at one portrait in particular.

'They hang these portraits like a badge of honour,' he said, 'So, they *hang forever.*' He mocked. 'Part cruel joke, part warning to stay in line.'

She didn't say anything.

He followed her eyes to the portrait.

'What happened to her?' Adiana asked with a lump in her throat.

Kace squinted and recalled the night, vividly, the green eyes of fear.

'She was a whore. And she was about the market square at night and got hanged for selling her body. Next to a dog.'

Adiana didn't move her eyes from the portrait, 'Did you see it? Her hanging?'

'I saw her the next day,' he said, 'hanging from the beam like a flour sack.'

Adiana's green eyes teared up, 'Did she look at peace?'

Kace felt the breath fall from him, 'She did,' he said gently.

Adiana turned to him and wiped away the tear bolting from her eyeball, 'Please, never call her a whore again.'

Kace shifted on his feet awkwardly, looking at the ground.

'I'm sorry.'

Adiana breathed out many years of stress. Then composed herself, 'Let's save our dog,' she said, her green eyes no longer fearful, but ablaze and concentrated.

They had managed to sneak out the back door and make it out without the crowd following them. The streets had a festival feel to them. He felt ill.

Kace paced around Adiana, who sat with a map of Ellon stretched out on the dining table.

'The town hall is here,' Adiana circled the building, 'where is the market square?'

Kace dropped his index finger on the space given to the square.

'So, they'll have to bring Elex along here and down this street to the square?' Adiana mapped out the route with her finger.

'It'll be dark,' Kace said, 'And he'll be heavily guarded.'

Adiana looked at the map solemnly, 'it's not very far, is it?'

Kace shook his head, 'It doesn't give us much opportunity.'

Just then, the sound of thick boots on the stairs outside came through the door. Kace walked towards the door and opened it to the sight of Sander standing looking awfully small in the doorway to his own home.

'Da...'

'Kace, may I come inside?'

'It's your house,' the boy said.

'I'll put the stove on,' Adiana said, standing to make herself useful, 'it seems odd to offer you tea in your own home?'

'Please,' said Sander to save her embarrassment. She went through the arched doorframe and into the kitchen.

'Thank you,' Kace cut through the silence, 'for what you said in court.'

'What little help it did,' he shrugged, feeling awkward and out of place, 'The king is a lot more powerful than me. Aye?'

Kace tapped the map, 'We're working on a plan. To break him free again.'

Sander shook his head, 'And run off a fugitive into

the forest again?' He looked sad now. 'Some battles can't be won.'

'Until there's a bullet fired,' Kace gulped, 'we haven't lost. And I am not giving up before then.'

Sander's tired old face flashed a snap of pride, 'I don't know where you got this determination from.'

Kace felt the compliment spread through him like a hit of energy while in a state of lethargy.

'It could only have been you and Má. I hardly saw anyone else, did I?' Kace teased.

Sander looked at the floor foolishly and Kace shook away the sympathetic pang he felt for his father.

'The route is short from town hall to market square,' Kace continued on as Adiana returned with a pot of hot tea for the crowd. Sander towered over the map, studying it.

He turned and walked to the window, the late afternoon was giving way to evening and bringing with it the end of Elex. He spoke quietly as if there was someone overhearing them.

'A few years back,' he said, 'there was a robbery. A cart carrying coins of tax from Ellon back to the King's town was ambushed. The robbers, out of towners so they were, had cut down a tree to block their planned route. And on the new route, the robbers lay in wait.'

'You're saying that's what we need to do?'

Sander turned back to them now, 'If we could put a diversion in place from the town hall to the market square, they'd be forced down a road they don't know.'

Kace looked down at the map, 'what sort of diversion would be enough?'

'How about a fire? A burning building.' Sander asked.

'We can't burn someone's house,' Kace looked up, 'perhaps a cart? If we steal a cart.'

Sander, sat at the table and pulled the map to him, 'this is the route,' he traced his finger along the two roads, and stopped at no place in particular, 'Kace, what is here?'

It took him a moment, but then he realised where his father's plump finger was rested. Kace looked up at his father, 'We can't.' He said sternly.

Adiana looked on confused, 'what is there?' She asked.

'If it's the best chance we have, boy…' Sander faded off, 'then so be it.'

'Da, I can't, we'll find another distraction. Some-how.' Kace said and scanned the map furiously, hoping an answer would jump up at him. Sander watched him, know-ing all too well that there was no other opportunity.

'No, we'll find another way.'

'Kace, listen to me. Burn it down. It's the only chance we have.'

Kace stopped searching the map and turned to the clueless Adiana. He looked helpless.

'What is there?' She asked.

'Da's workshop.' He replied.

'You don't have to do this,' Kace said as he, Sand-er and Adiana strode through the cobbled streets of Ellon, towards his workshop.

'I know, yet I want to.'

They walked into the little shop. As long as Kace had been alive, his father had run this little space. Making furniture at a reasonable price for local people. Huge carts of mass-produced products were coming in from across the water, yet, through it all, the little boutique shop had remained profitable.

'Plenty of wood to burn, aye.' Sander said, looking around at the dusty room filled with planks of wood along each wall and already made pieces chaotically about.

Kace opened his mouth to speak.

'Don't ask me if I'm sure,' Sander said, making the boy close his mouth quickly, 'because I am. It's time to burn the old to make way for the new.'

Kace had never felt prouder to carry the Di Comb name on. A fact he once used to hide, now formed a badge of honour.

'You know what ye are to do?' Sander said, showing Kace and Adiana to the door.

'Yes,' Adiana said back quickly, 'we'll be on the street over waiting.'

'When you see the smoke, it means it's nearing midnight,' Sander said, glancing at the clock on the wall.

They agreed where they were to meet after, should they be successful.

'And if we're not?' Kace asked gravely.

'We can't think like that,' Adiana said.

'Then,' Sander said, 'you can be proud that ye never gave up until the final moment.'

'That won't be much consolation.'

'Then let's not fail.'

Kace and Adiana slunk out of the workshop and into the darkened night. They found a small shop roof to climb up on and hid behind the arched dome atop it.

'There's only one way the procession can go once the fire has blocked them,' Kace reminded them, despite having talked about it at length already. 'Here. They must pass us here.' It was as if he was preparing for battle. 'We will drop down and demand they give us Elex.' He reached down and touched the barrel of his father's shotgun.

Adiana had been wary of the weapon.

'How else will we get them to hand Elex over?' Kace had asked.

'Why don't we come up with a cunning plan?' Adiana had pleaded.

'There's a time for wit, and there's a time for demanding what ye need,' Sander had said, 'now, with the dog's death imminent, all we have is the latter.'

Adiana had been reluctant, but without any alternative, she agreed on the basis that Kace was not to fire unless completely necessary.

'It's only to scare them,' she had said.

'Yes,' the father and son duo had said back.

They crouched for a long while as the night grew colder. They entertained themselves in a battle of who could blow cold mist out of their mouths the furthest.

They were lightheaded when the first sign of smoke came from the street over.

'He actually did it,' Kace said, reaching down and

picking up the shotgun.

They waited silently as the smoke grew taller and midnight came nearer. In the distance, they heard a series of voices.

'That must be them,' Adiana whispered. It was.

People moved towards the fire to see what all the commotion was about.

Fire, they heard through the dark night.

People shouted. Horses neighed. Feet ran. They couldn't tell what was happening.

Continue right, a voice shouted, and Kace peered over the ledge to see a dim light coming towards them.

As the light and its source neared, they could make it out more clearly.

The sheriff led it with a lantern, his men flanked a horse-drawn cart that had Elex, in his cage, on it.

'They're coming this way,' Kace whispered excitedly and cocked the gun.

'Be careful,' Adiana whispered back, pulling from her satchel a meat knife. Her protection.

'You too,' Kace said upon seeing the blade and its shine.

They were very near now. Kace and Adiana prepared to drop down in front of them. His heart raced. Hers did too.

The sheriff and his procession stopped suddenly. A quick halt followed by silence.

'What's happening?'

They looked down to see the men raising their guns slowly.

Kace and Adiana followed the line of their barrel to where at the end of the road, a dog stood before them. It growled, with its teeth on full display.

'Easy now,' the sheriff whispered to his men, 'get a clean shot.'

But the dog had started to run at them, far too fast to get a clean shot, and Elex had begun to bark wildly, too, throwing them all into a state of confusion.

Kace jumped from the ledge down to the street below.

'Ambush!' someone cried at the sight of the boy and his gun.

The horse carrying Elex had reared at the dog running towards it, and Elex's cage fell to the street, smashing open. The golden dog let out a slight whine as he tumbled. But then jumped free of his prison.

Adiana jumped down, too, and the sound of two vulgar gunshots cut through the still night.

Kace had fired one of them, it had hit one of the sheriff's men in the shoulder. Whereas the other one had come from the sheriff himself. Meant for the running dog, but instead, hitting a metal railing and ricocheting off into Kace's leg.

The pain was immense. He pulled up his gun, suddenly heavier now, and aimed it back at the men.

Elex, ran to Kace to check on him and then spun to bark angrily at the sheriff.

From behind, the unknown dog jumped on Elex, making him whine sharply. The unknown dog had Elex in its mouth by the scruff of his neck and was shaking the dog

wildly. Elex whined in pain.
The sheriff and Kace aimed their guns at different targets,
and one of them fired. Hitting and killing their target.
It was all silent then.

27.

The dog was dead.

Kace's arms trembled as he held the shotgun still fixed in place. The silence rang all around them.

Elex lay bleeding from his neck, his stomach inflating and deflating. Rise, fall. Rise, fall. A sweet sight in a bitter scene.

It took a moment for everyone to comprehend what was happening.

Kace's blood spilt from his leg and mixed with the feral dog's blood. Like two bloody rivers meeting at a lake.

After the commotion, Adiana had to do a double take on which dog had got shot, for they were both quite similar.

She saw Sander run to wrap his cloth top around the boy's bleeding leg. She ran towards Elex and used her satchel to press his neck wounds.

The sheriff took count, all his men were alive, just one writhed in pain on the floor. The sheriff turned, raised his handgun and put a bullet into the pained man's temple.

Everyone jumped at the sudden sound of the gun. Elex, wailed, unable to stand and run.

'What are you doing?' Another of his men cried out.

The sheriff placed a gun to that man's chest, 'he was going to die, I put him out of his misery.'

Unsure of whether to comply, the men started

to manoeuvre their guns into a ready position.

'Let me put a bullet in your chest and see if you want me to end it or die slowly,' the sheriff threatened, stiffening his men further. The sheriff waved his gun aimlessly about, 'I have no issue in killing any of ye if you don't go along with what happened here tonight.'

The sheriff paced in front of his men, grabbing the attention of Kace, Sander and Adiana too.

'This is what happened. Elex, the dog to be executed, escaped his cage, and in a struggle to capture him, we lost one of our men, and Elex was shot dead too.'

Everyone stared at him, confused. He hunched over Elex's weak body. 'You are dead,' he whispered and looked over at the dead feral dog. Then looked up at Kace.

'Do you understand? Run away from here. Go, take the dog with you and run.'

In the distance, the townspeople who had gathered in the market square were making their way up to the town hall.

'They will believe that this,' the sheriff said, pointing at the dead dog, 'is Elex. Take him away from here.'

Adiana pulled the bleeding Kace up to his feet, and Elex ascended painfully, too.

'Thank you,' Sander said, placing his big hand on the sheriff's shoulder.

Kace, Adiana, Sander and Elex hobbled off in the shadows. Under cover from the approaching crowd.

The sheriff turned to his men, alone now, 'They

are citizens of Ellon, it is our duty to protect them. Do you all understand? Anyone speaks of this, and I will make sure their family rots in my jail until the rats eat them.'

'How dramatic,' the soft voice said from behind him.

The sheriff turned, and there, looking so mundane, stood the king.

'Your Highness,' the sheriff bowed his head.

'Don't insult me with pleasantries now.'

'The dog is dead,' the sheriff said, pointing at the dead feral dog.

The king scoffed and kicked at the limp paws of the dog, 'This is not the dog.' He hissed, and then turned to his men, 'Go find the boy and his beastly dog.'

A loud gunshot rang, startling the king and making his men pull their weapons out.

The sheriff had shot a bullet high into the sky, 'Your Highness, I will not risk my reputation on this.'

'You have a lot more to worry about than your reputation,' the king said, 'You'll be begging for execution when my men have a go at you.'

From the far end of the cobbled street, the thick crowd was moving towards the spectacle.

To see the king standing in front of the town sheriff and bickering was absolutely unheard of.

'I will kill you, and I will burn your people!' The king spat angrily, unaware of how many people were now standing about. 'So, help me, I will deprive this town of everything. I am the king!'

He spun around to find the crowd morphing into a mob.

'Ye will not touch our sheriff,' a voice cried out, and the mob chorused similarly.

The king feigned a huge diplomatic smile, 'People of Ellon, I did not wish to speak so bluntly of you. But you must understand there is a threat to your town in the form of a dog. My men must get past you to find them.' He pleaded, his crown slipping off his head slightly as he begged.

The crowd didn't budge.

'Move, damn you!' The king cried, and turned to his guards, 'Move them!'

But his men didn't move, they were far too out-numbered. The whole of Ellon stood like a wall in front of them.

'Your Highness,' his head guard said, 'We can't…'

The king took the crown from his head, 'I will give a piece of this crown to anyone who will help me to capture that mutt!'

The crowd didn't even move a facial muscle.

'You must understand, Your Highness,' the sheriff said, 'Community is worth more than any jewel-studded crown.'

'I could make you all very rich in this town!' The king cried out helplessly.

Silence.

Until another brave voice spoke up from the back of the mob, 'Let the boy and his dog go free.'

The king, panting like a canine himself, stood small and unworthy, surrounded by the angry Ellon mob.

He turned to his guards weakly and pointed at the sheriff, 'Arrest him.'

That was the last thing the king had been able to say to his guards, for the mob rushed them and stripped them of their armour, weapons and clothes.

The king was left standing in the middle as his guards were beaten by the people of Ellon. No one touched the king, fearing how angry God might be. But they did snatch his crown and cloak amidst the brawl. They wore it mockingly. The poorest peasant of Ellon wearing a hat that cost more than he'd ever make in his life.

A crown is a silly thing, you see.

*

Kace limped with the help of Adiana, while Elex was being carried by the strong Sander.

'Where do we go?' Adiana cried.

'Stick with the original plan,' Sander said, the vein in his temple protruding with the effort of carrying the heavy dog.

They ran on towards the playing fields, over the wooden fence and into the thick forest.

Sander stopped dead in his tracks at his first glimpse of the house's turrets.

'Da,' Kace said softly, 'It's fine. Come on.'

Kace pulled Sander forward, and after a moment,

he followed. 'I haven't been here since that day,' he muttered to either the others or to himself.

'You'll be fine,' Kace pleaded with him, 'We have to get inside.'

The front door was kicked down by Sander's big booted foot. Kace and Adiana let him step in first. At the door, he rested Elex down like he was a sack of potatoes. The dog gave a little sigh and rested his sore head. Adiana helped Kace to a rotted velvet couch in the front room. He watched his father and his wet eyes looking around his old home.

'It must have been a beautiful place to live,' Kace said finally.

'It was your Ma's dream to be out here, ye see. She wanted away from Ellon. In the quiet. In the trees. She loved trees. And I needed them for work. So, we moved up here. People thought us weird. We were the tallest poppies in the field. But then, your brother died. Well, that moved us back down to Ellon, and made us conform. I guess that's what killed us.'

'It is a beautiful home,' Adiana said gently to Sander, who nodded.

'Aye, it is. Built it ourselves. Our dream home.' The tears were cascading now, and Kace and Adiana turned to each other, feigning a private discussion to give him some privacy.

They looked towards the sack of potatoes who lay breathing slowly by the door still.

'He looks like he lost a bit of blood,' Adiana said.

'You and me both, boy,' Kace said, wincing in

pain. Adiana walked over to Sander.

'I'm sorry to interrupt your moment, Mr Di Comb, but I think Kace might need a doctor.' She said, then looked at the dog at the door. 'And Elex might need a vet.'

Sander broke free from his stumble through memory lane and focused on the boy and the dog.

'The bullet is still in his leg,' Adiana continued, 'We can't risk it getting infected and killing him.'

'I know. I'm thinking.' Sander said. But there was no answer.

'I'm not going back down,' Kace said suddenly, 'To Ellon. It's not happening. I'm going to die a free man up here before I go down to a doctor.'

'If this is going to kill ye, I'm dragging ye arse down to Ellon meself.' Sander said, crossing the room to his son. Who looked weaker now that they'd rested for a moment.

'I'd rather die here than go back.'

And he was serious. Kace felt, for the first time, like he belonged in a place. Despite the bullet in his leg, he was comfortable. In the beautiful home once built by his parents long ago, with his Da and his two best friends.

'There's wood on the decking outside,' Adiana said, 'To start a fire.'

Sander smirked, 'telling me where the firewood is in me own house.' He stepped out to retrieve the wood.

Alone now, Adiana stroked Kace's hair, 'You aren't to die now on me, ok?'

Kace faintly smiled back, 'Aye, I'll do me best.'

Sander returned with an armful of wood and dumped it in the fireplace.

'I reckon I could get this place back into a bit of shape,' he declared to the room and began to build a structured pile.

'Elex…' Kace whispered.

'What?'

'Where has Elex gone?'

Adiana and Sander turned to the doorway where he had just been lying. It was empty now.

Kace tried to move, but the pain had made itself a home.

'Stay here, Kace.'

But there was not chance, he lifted himself up, grimacing in pain as he did, and Sander helped him out the door and around to the back garden.

The three humans stopped at the sight of the dog lying beneath the far tree.

'Elex…' Kace whispered.

But the dog did not move, he lay still with the most shallow of breaths.

Slow rises. Slow falls.

Kace didn't hear the voices. He was fixated on the dog at the bottom of the garden.

Sander and Adiana turned to see the sheriff climbing over the wall. But Kace did not see him at all. He was hobbling towards Elex.

'No…' He whispered, overriding the pain in his leg, 'You can't die on me. Please.'

Kace continued walking through the pain, the dog getting closer.

But he never got to him. His foot got caught on a creeper under the thick duvet of grass, and he fell forwards into blackness.

28.

A bullet can be challenging to remove from a boy's leg. Especially with how deep it was and how swollen the wound had gotten.

The surgeon worked for five hours until, finally, there was a high-pitched clink of the metal bullet in a metal bowl.

Adiana and Sander were sat by his hospital bed when he awoke. The last few memories were coming back to him sporadically. Little individual memories flashed by.

'Is Elex ok?' He asked groggily.

But they didn't need to answer.

As the boy saw, by his feet, Elex sat, panting with his big pink tongue hanging out.

He clambered along the small hospital bed, delicately avoiding Kace's injured leg, and lay himself in between the boy's torso and his arm.

'He looks well,' Kace said after cuddling the dog fiercely. Sander gave the dog a pat, too.

'He was given some cream for his wounds and antibiotics for any infection. They were unsure if to give him human or horse medicine. They opted for the former. Seems to have done the trick.'

'I guess he's more human than horse,' Adiana said, joining in on the pets.

'What happened?' Kace asked.

Sander cleared his throat and looked to the window like the sun was due to give him strength, 'there's been a revolution of sorts,' he began, 'the people of Ellon have stood up for the dog and us.'

Painfully, Kace sat up to listen. And they recounted what the sheriff had told them.

'What happens now?' Kace asked gravely.

Sander shrugged, 'Word is that more men are coming from the King's town in the coming days. Some are afraid, while some are looking for a brawl.'

'Are we in danger?'

'Who knows? They may not risk the civil unrest, they may not fight back. The king has been quiet since returning to his palace.'

'They may fear an attack on Ellon would look bad to all the neighbouring towns,' Adiana chipped in.

'And to lose control of their towns is the first sign of their demise,' Sander said, 'it's outdated, ye see. All this monarch stuff. Also, Ellon controls the majority of their fish trade. They can't risk losing that.'

'So, that's what it all comes down to? Playing politics.'

'That's all that separates us from the animals,' Sander said, 'Not our morals, nor our opposable thumbs. Just coin and politics.' He paused and stroked Elex's head, 'I think they have it better off.'

Kace couldn't help but again feel that warm sensation of home. A feeling he was becoming more used to. And one he was happy to meet. A friend with a smile.

PETER LAVERY

Epilogue

A sunny blue sky. A gentle breeze to cool the lick of sweat off one's body. A heavenly day.

Kace threw the stick, it flew high in the air and landed with a thud on the grass ahead. Elex bounded to it, picked it up and brought it back to Kace. Lying, obediently, waiting for the next throw. Hours of fun this was, for the dog.

Kace looked back at the decking, Adiana was sitting at the freshly varnished table, with her textbook out. It was a Saturday, but she still studied. She had declared she wished to study law at university, and Sander had spent a week's worth of coin on textbooks for her.

She and Kace were in the same class together at school. Kace still didn't enjoy school, bar one subject, biology.

'I want to be a vet when I'm older,' Kace had declared, taking Adiana's law spotlight, 'Adiana can sit there studying textbooks, and I'll play with Elex. That's my study.'

Sander officially adopted Adiana when she became a citizen of Ellon, and the three of them went about restoring the once-forbidden house.

Sander got a loan from the bank and stripped back his old life in the old house to make way for the new.

The insurance man paid out for his burnt-down workshop, and with that, he built a shed to run his business from home.

He had lobbied local representatives to build a

connecting road from the playing fields to their house. They had agreed, and the contractors had commenced work.

A law was passed within Ellon and its surrounding forest that dog hunting was to be banned.

They're clever things, dogs, and they began to come from far and wide when they realised that those in Ellon wouldn't kill them.

It had been awful tense at the start. Nervous dogs slunk into the town with nervous humans watching them. But they didn't bite. Neither human nor dog.

Soon, the dogs became comfortable, and the odd human took a particular liking to the odd dog. Less than a year after the night Elex was to be killed, dogs were living inside Ellon homes.

Having a dog by one's side meant being loyal and kind, and it became a symbol, rather quick.

I never trusted them before, but this little guy here, he's good company, ye know.

The King's town didn't bother Ellon any more. They kept away from their pro-dog rhetoric and focused on keeping their other towns sweet. Alas, word was spreading about the dogs of Ellon, and others were beginning to question the King's judgement.

And then, the story broke about how the king had trained a dog to cause havoc in Ellon, which was the final straw for most people in the land.

Perhaps, they pondered, dogs are only as bad as humans make them.

They began to flood to Ellon to see the tame dogs.

It wasn't long until even the royal family had to remove the decree to kill all dogs across the kingdom. Pressures from the people had forced their hand. The idea that many voices rule the land was born from how the dogs had been treated.

Eventually, the people would rise to demand that anyone could run to sit alongside the king and rule. It was to be decided by a public vote where the person with the majority of votes wins.

The idea was mocked at first, but so were Kace and his dog. And both became the norm quite quickly.

There was a female dog that visited Elex quite frequently, Kace and Adiana joked about how they were boyfriend and girlfriend, but once when Elex had been gone a long while so the two went looking for him.

'Elex!' They cried into the deep forest.

Adiana found them first, hidden beneath a bush, Elex, the female and a litter of puppies. All stumbling about their mother's nipples like pudgy little pocket-sized fur balls.

'Elex is a Da,' Kace said, marvelling at the row of pups.

'Congratulations to ye both,' Adiana said, shaking their paws respectfully.

They ran to fetch Sander, who decided to build them a little wooden kennel in the garden to call home.

Soon the garden was filled with two fully grown golden dogs and their eight puppies. And then the towns people saw their own dogs giving birth. The dogs, feeling safe and comfortable in Ellon, began reproducing rapidly.

These puppies were raised around tolerant humans and were not even slightly violent.

Of course, some lurked in the shadows and said it was wrong, we shouldn't accept them! God says it's wrong.

Those people found their voices were drowned out the more the public began accepting the dogs.

They would have toxic gatherings in secret, in deep dungeon bars, talking foul of the dogs.

Too many of them coming in, they'd say.

Most of those people were unhappy in their own lives and would go on to die alone. They'd spend hours hating the dogs until the stress of it got to them, while the dogs didn't even know of their existence. What a waste of a life.

Years went on, and Adiana left for university. She got a place to study law.

Kace remained at the house with Sander. His home workshop was more profitable than ever. Kace was shadowing a local vet, working long hours and loving it. He planned to be the first ever vet to specialise in dogs.

After a long day at a nearby stable, Kace returned home to find Sander sitting solemnly by the fireplace. Elex's little pups, now much older, bounded about the house, excited to see him.

'Are ye all right, Da?' Kace asked.

'I'm sorry, Kace.' He said, standing and hugging Kace hard. He didn't want to think what this could be. But deep down, he knew.

He followed Sander out to the decking.

There at the end of the garden, by the tall oak tree, Elex lay motionless.

Kace took small steps towards the dog that appeared only to be sleeping. He hunched down by the dog's side and stroked his long fur.

Kace knew this day would come soon. He was a good age, that dog.

'You were, are and always will be my best friend,' Kace whispered to the dog as his eyes began to rain.

'You will forever be the most important thing to ever happen to dogs. The day in the forest when you walked over and sniffed my hand. You changed history. And you'll never understand that. But you did. You changed this entire kingdom. What an impact. What a life worth having.'

Sander took a shovel and began to dig an Elex-sized hole by a baby Danyan tree in the garden.

Kace leant to its trunk and whispered; *I hope that dogs will forever be a man's best friend.*

PETER LAVERY

THE DOGS OF ELLON

ABOUT THE AUTHOR

Born in Dublin, Ireland, Peter is a young writer and filmmaker. From a young age, he opened a multitude of businesses, starting in nightclub promotion before moving into the hospitality industry.

In 2019, he moved to London, UK in order to dedicate himself fully to his passion for storytelling, and graduated with a BA in Practical Filmmaking from the MetFilm School in 2022.

In 2021 Peter became a multi-award winning writer & director for his short narrative film Tequila Dream.

His writing has been described as *witty, poignant* and *sensitive*.

He currently lives in London where he tries to write, but mostly just stares out the window at passing dogs.

ACKNOWLEDGEMENTS

This book would not have been written without Niamh by my side constantly asking for my word count. Thank you for reading the first 10K and telling me to keep going.
Love always x

Aimee for your insight and skill on the edit.
All my family and friends for everything always, you know who you are.

AUTHOR'S PHOTO: JOE ANDREWS
COVER DESIGN: SARA DIOMAIUTO